I0571031

EXES ON THE BEACH

Hope Izzati

Exes on the Beach

Hope Izzati

ISBN: 978-1-5272-0032-6

Published by Bronwyn Editions in the UK 2016

Cover artist: D M Samson

1

Nancy Niven had split up with boyfriends for all the usual reasons; infidelity (on both sides), incompatibility, boredom, domestic violence, relocating abroad, excessive drug use. But never, ever, in her life did she think she would part company with a man because of the singer, Shirley Bassey.

A few days afterwards, sitting in her rented apartment in Brooklyn, waiting for a girlfriend to go to lunch with, she had computed all the other factors involved in the parting of the ways - that he was a control freak, billionaire property developer, twenty four years her senior, with three ex-wives, high blood pressure and a terrible temper.

'Who the fuck is this Shirley Bassey broad?' he had asked, at the wheel of his black Porsche Panamera, as they cruised through the Upper East Side of Manhattan.

'What!?' she had asked, playfully aghast. 'Only an icon. A diva.

One of the greatest singers ever.'

'Never heard of her. Don't put her on.'

The argument started from there. Nancy loved cars, from her cute Fiat 500, back at the family home in West London, to the Mercedes B-Class she drove for work in New York City. She loved Porsches, but her feelings towards them would always now be tainted by that blazing row. At first, she tried to win him over to Ms Bassey's amazing talent, leaning coquettishly across onto his right thigh, which she knew he liked, giving him the doe-eyes, through indignation at how firm he was being, all the way through raised voices, until she saw his raging temper for the first time. On reaching her apartment building, she had actually exited the Porsche while it was still moving a little, leaving him with a, "Knobhead!" and a slammed door.

Nancy shook the bad thoughts from her head as she padded across the polished wooden floor to her kitchen for a glass of water, looking intensely at her two work cell phones. Damn, she thought. She was waiting for an offer to be made. *Oh, come on! Come on. Ring.*

Right above the stove sat a tile mosaic, made for her by a designer friend, which depicted the outline of Indonesia in bright green. It took everyone's eye on entering the kitchen, and alluded to the fact that 26-year-old Nancy was half Indonesian and half English, born in Jakarta in 1990. Her English father had been very handsome (still devilishly was, in her eyes) and mother a gorgeous local woman, so Nancy was ravishingly sultry, with black hair, black eyes, not too tall, as mother was only five foot herself. She looked at herself in a wall mirror, checking her outfit of white blouse and pale-blue skinny jeans, ripped open at the knees. Being petite, she had to watch her weight, and she wondered if her bottom was getting a little bit big. No, it was as cute as ever.

Nancy sipped water, while looking out the window, although there wasn't much of a view, just neighbouring buildings and the road. There came the expected rap on the door - friend, Gabby, only lived on the floor above. Maybe the important call would come while they were at lunch.

'Noooooo!?'

'Yessss, I'm telling you.'

Nancy and Gabby were seated in the Morris Sandwich Shop on Lincoln Place. Gabby was an old family friend, with dual US and British nationality, currently working in New York as a nanny to the family of a rich banker. She was a blonde, happy-go-lucky person, occasionally prone to bimbo-style behaviour, but had been a great help to Nancy's relocation.

After college, Nancy had worked at an Estate Agents office in Twickenham, South West London. It was due to her obsession with the Channel Four TV property show, *Location, Location, Location*, and not meant to be her main career. But after proving to be a friendly, competent agent, who actually took personal interest in her clients, rather than going through the motions, and making a lot of money in the process, a colleague decided she would do well in a New York agency that a mutual friend was attached to. Nancy loved New York from family holidays, so she followed through on it very seriously indeed.

'No,' repeated Nancy, all agog. 'He didn't?'

Gabby sucked on her straw, grinning. 'He did.'

'What did you do?'

'I let him, of course.'

The two friends screamed with laughter and joined hands over the table. Finally their hilarity settled down and Nancy, blushing a little and her fantastic smile fixed in place, paid attention to her meal.

'How's the million dollar listing job going this week, then?' asked Gabby.

Right on cue, one of Nancy's cell phones rang, to the tune of an old British cop show called *The Sweeney*. Gabby recognised it and smiled. Nancy was up and excusing herself - she was waiting for an offer on an apartment which would give her the biggest commission since starting as a Real Estate agent in the city. She was expecting the buyer's broker, but the caller ID told her it was her boss, Daniel Bridgford. She stepped outside, brushed her unruly hair back from her forehead and answered, 'Daniel?'

'Hello, Nancy. We've had an offer on the condo in Chelsea.'

'Really? Why wasn't I called?'

'Now don't panic. Instead of the one unit, the buyer wants the whole building.'

Nancy's heart leapt. 'The whole building?' She hadn't even worked out the commission on something like that. She giggled down the phone. 'Hehehehehe.'

Daniel sounded pleased for her. 'I thought you'd be happy. I shall expect you in the office as soon as, then?'

'Yes! Yes, Daniel. I'll be there soon. Thank you. Thank you!'

A flat in Luton, Bedfordshire

"Poo in the kettle!"

Annie Dyer roared with laughter, almost dropping her Kindle Fire into the bathwater. She was reading hotel reviews on Trip Adviser. Standing next to her, brushing his teeth, was Jason Ikin, a handsome, 26-year-old builder and amateur rugby player. He was naked and turning so he could see the initial outline of his new left shoulder tattoo, which he planned to get finished before he and his girlfriend went on holiday.

'*What?*' he asked, looking down at her.

Annie giggled. 'Don't, whatever you do, stay in this hotel. "I wish I could give it negative stars."' She scrolled down further. '"What a shithole."'

Jason leant down on the pretence of reading the screen, but instead sucked on her left nipple.

'Jason! Toothpaste on my nipple now.'

'Have we decided yet, babe? I fancy Tenerife this year.'

He played with her brunette ponytail, giving consideration to getting into the tub with her. The phone rang in the hallway. Annie handed him the Kindle, so she could get on with bathing. He left the machine on the table in the hall as he answered the phone. Quickly he returned to the bathroom.

'Who was it?' asked Annie.

'They asked if I was Jason Ikin, then hung up.'

Annie laughed. 'Bailiffs checking up on you.'

Jason assessed her soapy body. 'The only thing I've got of any value is you.'

'Aww, baby.'

She started to fondle his balls. A mischievous grin spread across her face. Instantly he became aroused. With a little splash she was in position, going down on him but still connecting with her hazel eyes.

'You'd fetch a couple of hundred quid at auction,' he appraised.

Mock fury came over her and his cock was ejected. Still she held his testicles and her grip had become much firmer.

'Careful, mister, when I've got you like this.'

Discomfort made him giggle and apologise and force his way into the tub and on top of her. A little water was displaced. She was laughing again and then they were kissing madly.

2

Daniel Bridgford sat with a glass of diet coke and a grilled chicken sandwich in his favourite bar, around the corner from the Crow East Real Estate office, where Nancy Niven worked under him. He tapped his mouth with a napkin. His face was quite tanned, from a recent game of tennis. He was a handsome man, who had been in the business for nearly twenty years, first in his home state of Connecticut, and was doing quite well for himself. He owned a penthouse duplex in Soho, with a view of the Empire State Building, and dated an ex-model, Ulrika, although she spent a large part of the year in her native Sweden. So, life was marvellous yet his mood that morning touched on the melancholic, having found his first grey chest hair. At first he had been shocked at how overly sensitive he felt about it. After all, he already had a flash of distinguishing grey at the temples. At thirty-nine it was bound to happen sooner or later, just... there... on his manly chest, which he worked on religiously in the gym, it really got to him. He shook the nonsense from his mind again and got ready to head back to the office.

'You!' said a striking blonde woman, standing there, instantly taking the full attention of about eight businessmen, plus the bartender. '...are coming away with me on a long, dirty weekend, right this second.'

Not something heard every day of the week.

After a pause, Daniel sighed audibly, put on a hangdog expression and made to move as instructed, then he laughed with the man next to him, who patted him on the back, clearly the partner and object of desire for this funny lady. Daniel sat back down, grinning, thoroughly cheered up. He watched the lucky guy leave with his smart woman. He shook his head and checked his watch; he would ring Ulrika before his first meeting of the afternoon.

Ulrika hadn't answered, which made him absent-mindedly mess with the buttons on his shirt as he entered the foyer of the Crow East offices, thinking of his chest hair again. After nodding to the Concierge, he took the elevator up to the open-plan second floor, where he could see his secretary, Jean, talking to... Jesus Christ! Gus Kaitiff was a full thirty minutes early. *Shit.* And not even made comfortable in his office, with no coffee cup in hand, standing in reception. And with a West Highland terrier at his feet. *What was with the West Highland terrier?* Daniel glared pleadingly at Jean, then his face was all friendly as Gus turned to him. Daniel looked at one of his most important clients. He thought the deal for the

Chelsea building was cut and dried from their recent phone call, even if Nancy Niven had hit the roof. He had warned her not to get involved with the powerful man. But what could he do now, apart from go along with the man's plans in all good faith.

'Gus! Hello. You're a little early.'

'Daniel, sorry about that. Jean's been a treasure, looking after me, but... well, look at Milly here. Just look at her.'

Daniel looked at the dog.

'She's sick, Daniel. We have to go to the vets.'

'The vets?'

'Yes, Daniel, the vets.'

Nancy Niven wore grey sweat pants and a University of St Andrews tee-shirt, although she had never been to Scotland. The trouble with Scotland, she thought, as she looked at herself in the reflection from the window, is that... it's full of Scots. She was on her punch bag in the spare room – the room which had a view of the side of the building next door. She put in a few punches, trying and failing to remember where that Scottish quote came from. Which boyfriend had gone to that university? None. Most were too stupid for further education. Then she remembered, the shirt had belonged to a friend of her sister. She missed kid sister, Lucy. Maybe she should book a vacation home?

Nancy felt wired, flushed and sweating. Two days since rushing to see Daniel, since hearing the amazing news of her selling a whole building, since hearing that her Ex, Gus Kaitiff, the man with the temper, was the man behind the deal. Gut-wrenching. Total anti-climax. Why had he taken it over? Why? Only two reasons; either to force her to work closely with him, or to pull it all away from her at any time, whenever he could get the most sadistic enjoyment from it. It was awful. Her pulse had not calmed down since. Stupid! Stupid girl. Stupid to mix business with pleasure. She should have listened to Daniel. Now she felt totally insecure. She was a tough cookie but she suddenly wanted her mummy.

But time to keep going. She had other listings to deal with. Maybe if she could close some other deals quickly then she could cope with whatever Gus was playing at. Her figures were still exceptional for a fairly new broker. And Daniel would stand up to Gus if anything unprofessional started to go down. She breathed deeply, threw off her training gloves and headed to the shower, thinking about her first listing appointment of the day. It was with a man called Richard who was selling his apartment in Tribeca and moving to LA. Her PA, the lovely Zach, remembered him from a previous move, describing a drop-dead gorgeous hunk to her, and bemoaning the fact that he was straight. Under the hot jet, Nancy thought it would be perfect to spend a bit of time with a handsome man, knowing he was leaving town and not likely to ever cross her path again. Men!

It was clearly the wrong Richard. This man was about sixty, skinny and bespectacled, retired from the pharmaceutical business, with his wife, Helen, saying hello from the kitchen. Nancy let him show her round the apartment before sitting down to discuss finances. Helen came through with tea on a tray, and they sat there pleasantly, with the conversation moving to why they were relocating.

'Oh, it's time to be near our grandkids,' said Helen.

'That's so wonderful,' said Nancy. 'What better reason?'

It really was nice. What a lovely couple. Just what Nancy needed to calm her nerves and remind herself that it didn't all have to be about cold, hard cash and sharks in the water.

'Our son has a farm just outside Los Angeles,' added Richard. 'We can have a garden again after thirty years of being in New York. We love it here, don't get me wrong, but it's time to get out.'

'I understand,' said Nancy.

The talk moved to Nancy's background, her accent, as it usually did at listing appointments. They were intrigued to hear about her exotic heritage. Once the tea was drunk and Richard's signature dry, Nancy bid them farewell, and went down to her Mercedes. She answered a few voicemails. She checked her appearance in the rear-view mirror. Next.

Milly the West Highland terrier was on Daniel Bridgford's lap. They were in Gus Kaitiff's Porsche heading to the vets' office.

'Daniel, I'm worried.'

'The dog doesn't seem too distressed to me.'

'Not about Milly. That's just a touch of diarrhoea.'

Daniel digested that startling piece of information. 'Then what are you worried about, Gus?'

'I'm worried about Nancy.'

'Nancy Niven? Gus, I assure you Nancy will act in a very professional—'

'I'm sure she will. No, no, I'm worried that she is close to burn-out. You pressure your people too much. I know the kind of business we're in, but Nancy is special. You need to handle her better.'

'Yes, Gus.'

'After this Chelsea deal you need to give her some time off.'

'Excellent idea. I should have thought of it myself.'

'You just did. Don't you have a villa in the Caribbean?'

'Not the last time I spoke with my accountant.'

'Well, I do. She needs to spend some time there away from it all.'

'Gussssssss...'

Gus checked on Milly. 'Nearly there, baby.' Then to Daniel, 'My daughter dotes on Milly. Listen, Daniel, you mustn't worry. I have a massive amount of business to put your way. I'm genuinely worried about Nancy. I've had three wives, remember. It will do her the world of good. All the time she's in the Caribbean I will be in and out of your office. You have my word. Let's make this happen. I want to work closer with Crow East Real Estate, and so do all my business contacts.'

'Gussssssss...'

'Now, Daniel...'

'Gus, I'm now concerned with what Milly's doing.'

'Really? Well, shit. Don't sweat it, we're nearly there.'

3

The sign on the side of the white Transit van read: *Ikin Plumbing and Heating. Luton, London, Paris and New York. But mainly Luton.*

Jason Ikin and his older brother, Neil, were fitting a new bathroom at a detached property on the road that led to Whipsnade Zoo; they did tend to grasp at any novelty to break up the monotony of tiling a shower or fitting a sink. During the first tea break, Jason found a GIF on his phone of a monkey grabbing a hyena by the tail, before running away, only to sneakily return to grab a leg. They both found it hilarious. But the Ikin brothers always did a professional job doing floors, ceilings and electrics, and leaving everywhere spotless. It had led to many word-of-mouth recommendations, and that was why they were out there, on a sunny day, with their radio blaring, and both working in just their jeans and boots, with the posh, elderly customers out at work.

As Neil jig-sawed wood on the driveway, which was to go on the floor of the en-suite, Jason loaded more rubbish into the skip. He was sweating, glistening. He took a moment to enjoy a nice breeze. He was ready for his fish 'n chips lunch. He just needed to finish that... Suddenly, a loud wolf whistle came from a passing car. Jason bent forward to be able to see inside the moving Citroen. It was a well-dressed, middle-aged woman, smiling broadly. Jason gave her a grin and a little wave and then watched the car turn the corner.

'Was that for you or me?' asked Neil.

'Definitely for you, bro'.'

'I'll take it. I'll take everything I can get these days.'

Jason sat on a low wall to watch his brother finish the final floor panel. He stretched himself out, after being in the confined en-suite for an hour, making his impressive back muscles ripple.

'Is it lunchtime, then, Neil?'

'Aye, I think so. Has Annie failed to do your sandwiches again? Where is she today?'

Annie Dyer, Jason's girlfriend, was an air stewardess, working short-haul out of Luton Airport.

'Düsseldorf, I think.'

'Düsseldorf? Arrrgh, German beer. Think of that. Right, kid, I'll get off to that chippy we spotted, then.'

'Okay, mate.'

Jason took the flooring upstairs and finished it off. Then he went down to the rear garden to await his lunch, sitting in the shade. He thought about Annie, and their six months together. She was amazing. So prim and proper in her uniform, and so dirty out of it. There had been five girlfriends in his life, less than people would assume – for such a hottie (if he did think so himself). If he was the kind of guy to make up some kind of rating scale, then Annie would be top in four or five groups: she would be top in blow jobs, for sure, but bottom in anal (which she wasn't into) and that was a worry. He realised that an attractive neighbour had come out to pin washing to the line. The woman was thirty-something, long brunette hair, in jeans and a tight tee-shirt which showed off her great figure. He imagined... Then he looked away, grinned and scratched his head, even yawned a bit. Where on earth was his fish 'n chips lunch!?

Nancy Niven had a habit of stopping anywhere once her cell rang, then holding it out in front of her face like a prop from *Star Trek*. She didn't care if people had to give her a wide berth – she was in New York to make money, not be polite. It was great to meet older people like Richard and Helen, or couples with young children, but she wanted to make herself financially secure before Mr Right came along, and then babies followed in leafy Surrey.

She took the call from a Mr Rooney on a recommendation from a previous client. A sour-faced, old woman tutted as she had to deviate around Nancy to enter a store, while a man looked her up and down, perhaps liking her black business suit or her wild Indonesian hair blowing in the wind. Mr Rooney was selling his apartment and, after a quick think, Nancy realised she was within a block of him and arranged to go there immediately.

Bizarrely, on the brief walk, Nancy somehow managed to get a strain in her right calf. And the wind had been blowing straight at her, so she was huffing a bit as she gathered herself in the entranceway to Mr Rooney's building. Through the shadows of the plate glass window she spotted a man crossing the foyer and just knew he had come down to meet her. How typical. How inconvenient. Hastily, she tried to gather her hair and find a way to walk without limping as he opened the door.

'Miss Niven? Hi, I'm Leo Rooney. Come in, out of the weather.'

Nancy shook his hand. Oh, good God, she thought, as her eyes followed the hand all the way up a full arm sleeve of multi-coloured tattoos (she liked a tattoo on a man but until that moment had been against the extreme craze of going over the top) and the other arm was the same, with black and red and a touch of yellow, and... speechless... his neck was the same, and if he removed his white vest from his rock hard chest then his body would be the same... and at the same time she was dealing with the whitest and warmest smile ever, lovely blue eyes, chiselled cheekbones, a little scar before his fair crew cut started. Something had caused her to go mute, total brain freeze. She realised it was the combination of a completely tattooed man, which suited him, and the gentle, sexy voice. She found a smile herself and gestured at the gusty weather to explain her flustered state.

'Come up,' he said. 'The first floor. I have coffee on.' They started to walk. She felt like someone had shot her leg with a paintball gun.

'Lucky you were in the neighbourhood.'

'Yes, wasn't it.'

Carry me, damn you! her mind screamed. Carry me! What an extraordinary man. And that smell! That aftershave. She could feel his scent invading her bra and panties, his bare hand moving it around on her body. He was talking again.

'I'm hoping to find somewhere nearer my studio in Harlem. I'm a photographer.'

Imagining him photographing her nude body, Nancy determined to become professional, taking a deep breath, and as soon as she stepped over the threshold she began appraising the apartment's assets. Yet still she sneaked glances at him. He was not built up like a body-builder, just naturally fit and muscular. What would her mother think about the neck tattoo? *Screw mother*.

'Seen enough?' he asked, handing her a cup of coffee.

'I sold the unit above last month. I'm sure I can get you the figure you're looking for.'

He was rubbing the back of his neck, stretching his ribcage even more. Those blue eyes twinkled. 'The figure I'm looking for? Sounds great.' He gestured for her to sit on the couch, where he joined her.

Nancy tucked hair behind her right ear, and immediately berated herself for doing that tell-tale action. She needed to sit there and get her thighs together as she actually felt herself becoming moist. He never stopped smiling.

'So what price have you in mind?' he asked.

Maybe he is smiling about the potential sale, she thought,

rubbing her thighs together.

'May I call you Nancy?' he asked, before she could answer.

'Please do. Well, Mr Rooney...'

'Then it must be Leo. Nancy, I'm trying to place your accent.'

'Indonesian-English. So, Leo. Short for..?

'Leonard.' He laughed. 'Got you there, everyone expects Leonardo.'

She was soaking her panties, even for the Leonard.

4

Over the weekend, Nancy needed to be alone, and she needed to drink a lot of her favourite red wine. Nancy was not a Muslim, much to many people's surprise when she said she was half-Indonesian. Instead, her mother's family came from the smaller Christian community, although Nancy was not in the least religious and, in her teenage years, had drunk like a trooper.

She turned down a restaurant trip with two friends in the office, declined the movies with Gabby from upstairs, and took a rain check with a sexy broker she had given her number to recently at an Open House event. Instead, she ordered in Chinese food and finally started watching *The Tudors* on box set. She lounged around in her pyjamas while emailing family back in England (she always found Skype to be completely, utterly fucking useless). She masturbated herself in the shower while dreaming about the tattooed Mr Leonard Rooney.

She found time to start reading the first Kurt Wallander novel, about the Swedish police detective (bought because Daniel Bridgford's partner was Swedish), and checked her GoodReads account, where her talented cousin, Jane's romantic novel had two thousand ratings, at an average of 4.20, which seemed respectable. Not exactly Jodi Ellen Malpas, but not too shabby.

And all weekend she fretted about the Gus Kaitiff situation. At some stage, perhaps after her third glass of wine, she realised that what she disliked most was injustice – she worked damn hard at her job and deserved everything she got. She hated having the fear of failure hanging over her head just because a relationship had failed. It was just plain wrong.

A chaperone! That was it. Nancy's father always used to say there was an answer to every problem. So she came up with the idea of always having a chaperone during her meetings with Gus, over negotiations on the building in Chelsea. And who better than Zach, her Crow East office PA? Her adorable, barely competent, best friend in the office.

First thing Monday morning, he sat in the passenger seat of her Mercedes, as they headed to Gus Kaitiff's office, like a prisoner given parole, eyes wide for all the people out and about on Madison Avenue. He was in a pale blue suit and held a small leather man-bag on his lap. Nancy thought those bags had appeared and disappeared overnight, about ten years ago, but there was one, right there. Zach smiled at her. She wanted to adopt him.

They took the elevator up to the penthouse office and were welcomed by Gus's secretary, Mia, a fifty-something lady with a hint of plastic surgery around her eyes. Nancy could sense Zach's need to point the fact out to her as soon as he got the chance. Mia was pleasant enough and made them comfortable, until Gus was free. They politely declined coffee.

Sitting, looking at the magnificent view, Nancy realised that Zach had taken hold of her hair at the back of her head and was tugging lightly. 'What *are* you doing?'

'I'm seeing what you'll look like with a face-lift.'

She was happily astonished at him. 'Will you behave? Jeez, I give you a day out...'

Zach giggled.

The ornate double doors to Gus Kaitiff's office swung open and the man himself stood there, framed against the blue skyline. He wore an open-necked shirt. His salt and pepper hair was slicked back. There was a massive gold watch on his wrist. Nancy did like an older, handsome man, and Gus was certainly impressive. But she knew she didn't like him one bit any more, she just wanted this deal closed.

'Nancy, lovely to see you.'

They both stood up. Zach was nervously anticipating a handshake that wasn't forthcoming, causing him to sulk a little bit. Gus stood aside to let them enter his office. Nancy was in two minds whether to play it cool and listen to his demands or to start talking fast and try to get matters moving along. She was stopped dead to find Daniel Bridgford standing there.

'Daniel?' she queried, staring at him.

'I brought Daniel here early,' interjected Gus. His hand brushed her back in passing. 'We thought it best to close the deal on the Chelsea building without any further ado. Congratulations, Nancy, it's your biggest success so far.'

'I don't understand,' said Nancy, looking at an equally puzzled Zach, then back at Daniel, who remained po-faced. 'Daniel? I thought there were issues needing resolving before the sale could go through?'

'All swept away,' said Gus, very expansively. 'It's done, Nancy. I wish you all the best with all your future listings. Drinks! We must celebrate.'

As Gus began to open a bottle of Krug champagne, Nancy moved to Daniel.

'We'll talk later,' Daniel said quietly. 'Everything's signed. Everything's good, believe me.'

Nancy felt such relief that she would not have to negotiate on anything with Gus that she accepted a flute of champagne. She sipped it but declined to take part in the men's glass clinking or laughter.

'What the fuck is that?' joked Gus, noticing Zach's bag.

Zach looked down at his bag, pretending to be mildly offended. 'It's my bag.'

Gus laughed louder, so Daniel and Zach laughed with him. Nancy found a place to put her glass of champagne down.

By coincidence, the wide-open, public playing fields where Jason Ikin and his rugby mates did their training was right behind his and Annie's rented flat. It was not uncommon for her and her friends to lean out of the window and make unladylike comments towards the men. The latest training session was taking place in a force ten gale, and she was out shopping, anyway, so the guys went about their practice without being heckled. Lots of boisterous tackles flying in and cheery banter. Jason was head to toe in mud, glancing up at his apartment window, as if Annie would lean out with a sign saying she had booked Tenerife for their holiday and he should come home immediately.

Their Coach called time on the session, and all the men headed to the sports facility buildings, desperate for a shower and an energy drink. One guy had his mate in a headlock, two others were play-fighting, some discussing their planned night out. They all hit the showers. So much testosterone and tattoos. Only the night before, Annie had asked him if she could be the team's physiotherapist. Cheeky mare, he had called her.

'Yeah, too much snooker on TV these days,' scrum half Tony was saying next to him. 'What's with British Eurosport? When they show snooker all we can hear is the auditorium's air-conditioning. Drives me nuts.'

'Just got that BT Sport, myself,' said Coach. 'Trying to get into baseball. It's very odd.'

'My missus wants to take up tennis with me,' said hooker,

Waheed, shampooing his head like mad.

'Fucking tennis?' asked flanker, Darren. 'What's all that bollocks of asking for the fucking towel after every fucking point? Eh? Tell me fucking that.'

Jason grinned. Annie had played some Junior tennis around the country while a schoolgirl. He started to think about her – not recommended to start fantasising about girlfriends while in the shower with sixteen other men. Nevertheless, he washed his groin religiously so he would be good and fresh for her later.

'I was with that Tina in the Red Lion last night,' Tony was saying. 'She's after a gesture of commitment from me. Listen, Tina, love, I said, I tell you what, listen to this, I'd wax my shoulders for you, babe.'

Amid the groans, one person did laugh at that. Jason was done, towelling down, checking the new tattoo again in a mirror. He could not wait to get to Annie.

5

'Daniel, but I'm fine.' Nancy laughed. 'I'm over it, I promise you.'

'It was a very... stressful time, Nancy... you need a break... you should take a vacation.'

'But, Daniel, I've almost closed on Leo Rooney's apartment... and I have several other irons in the fire.'

Nancy was getting dizzy, watching a whirl of white suits running in a circle in front of her. Daniel Bridgford was involved in a Tae-Kwon Do lesson, in the basement of his friend's building: an airless tomb that felt like an oven and had the twenty students gasping and sweating profusely. They were being led in a jog around the room by their Master Instructor, a red-haired man who went by the name of Big Ronnie, and hailed from Alabama. Nancy shared a smile with Big Ronnie. The man was clearly insane and taking great pleasure in torturing his students, with two or three at the back about to be lapped.

Big Ronnie stopped at Nancy, but waved his students to continue. He insisted Nancy took a bottle of mineral water from the mini-fridge and they both stood there chatting. Big Ronnie might be an intimidating, 260lb martial art, Black Belt, but he was obviously quite shy around the gorgeous, delicate Nancy.

'When are you going to join my class, Miss Nancy?'

'Ronnie, darling, I wish I had the time.'

'But imagine the deals you could make if you could kick the other broker in the head.'

'Oh, I have. I have, believe me.'

They both giggled and bounced shoulders off each other.

'You look tired in the eyes, Nancy. If you don't mind me saying so? Are you eating properly?'

'I think so.'

Big Ronnie accepted that, then turned to his students. 'And... stop!'

The students desperately stumbled to a halt. Two of them asked permission to get water and were refused. One looked about to vomit.

'Put the pads and mitts away, then we'll do some cool-down stretches.' Then to Nancy, 'You may sit alongside Daniel, seeing as you are my favourite.'

'Aw, and you're my favourite too, Ronnie.'

Nancy went to Daniel and he did a comedy fall right in front of her. Nancy giggled and sat next to him, even taking part in the cool-down stretches. She could easily touch her toes, while Daniel was bemoaning the state of his groin.

'I've had pressure from above,' gasped Daniel.

'Really?'

'You've been tetchy recently. Someone even queried whether you were right for Crow East.'

'Oh.'

'So, Nancy, take the company jet, spend a week with your toes in the white sand.'

'Daniel, I was thinking of going home.'

'No! I mean, no, then you would just take on board family matters. Further stress. You need isolation. You need to find yourself.'

'I need to find myself?'

'Well, no, but I've always wanted to say that.'

They both laughed. Nancy copied Big Ronnie and pushed her knees open and down to the side and found no resistance, unlike Daniel who grimaced and complained about his groin again.

'How's Ulrika?'

'She flies in from Stockholm tonight. All her business resolved. I've really missed her.'

Nancy smiled. 'I'm sure you have. Okay, Daniel, I'll just close the Leo Rooney sale and then I'll take the vacation.'

'That's my girl.'

To Nancy's delight, the Leo Rooney sale turned into a two-person bidding war, so she had to keep calling him with the increased offers. He took great amusement from it, asking at one point when it would stop so he could actually go ahead and move home. When a final offer did come in, and it wasn't subsequently beaten, she arranged to meet the man, but to add to the mix, her sister, Lucy, had decided to come over the pond on a mini-break. It was the girl's first time in America, so there had to be visits to all the usual tourist sights, and although Nancy was only dealing exclusively with Leo, the week seemed as busy as ever.

The day arrived where she was having lunch with Lucy and then dinner with Leo later. The sisters caught up with all the news of family life back home, and with Lucy's future career plans. Nancy withheld details of Leo Rooney, although not clear exactly why. It was not as if she had only ever dated shy, nice boys. Compared to Lucy she was the black sheep of the family, occasionally rebellious, a little selfish, not bad but no goody-two-shoes either. Once, Lucy had asked her along to help with a charity cake baking event. Nancy had been so bored that she had actually walked out on it, causing a big row later at home.

Lucy was currently single, which perhaps explained why there had been no instant talk about men from the moment she had walked through the Arrivals Hall at JFK. But that was nice, just two sisters spending time together. Then out of the blue, over coffee, Lucy mentioned Jason Ikin. Nancy looked up sharply. That was a touchy name to her. Her first boyfriend. It had not ended too well, mainly down to herself (her moody, illogical teenage self) but the final nail in the coffin had been his infidelity with her best friend.

They had managed to be civil on the few occasions they had bumped into each other since, at weddings and in bars around town.

'He was fitting a friend's kitchen,' explained Lucy. 'I had a shock when I recognised him. He's filled out a bit.'

'What do you mean, filled out a bit? Fat?'

'No, silly. Hunkywise.'

'That's not even a word.'

'Whoarrrr, then. That's a word. I think he's a rugby player now.'

'Was he well?'

'Yeah. He was dead nice to me. I always liked him, at school. I don't know why you treated him so appallingly.'

'*Lucy!*'

'I'm teasing.'

'Did he ask about me?'

'Of course. He was genuinely impressed with news of what you're doing over here.'

'Is he seeing anyone?'

'I didn't ask. I remember the room was full of dust, so it was quite brief. A brief look at him in his vest.'

Lucy was happy to be left alone in Nancy's apartment that evening, quite looking forward to good pizza and American TV (even with the insane advert breaks). Nancy spent an hour getting ready for Leo, showering and then shaving within an inch of her life. She was so excited, thinking of his inked muscles and piercing blue eyes, but also guilty over her sister. What if matters moved on? Would Lucy be okay alone overnight? So she determined to play hard-to-get with Leo. After all, having Lucy there was the perfect excuse. That was the plan, keep him keen for her return from vacation, all refreshed and windswept.

Leo buzzed from downstairs at eight o'clock, prompting a playful wrestling match between the two sisters as Lucy pretended that she expected to vet the man. Nancy forced the smaller Lucy back inside the apartment, kissed her and skipped downstairs.

Leo Rooney was in a designer white tee-shirt, and dark blue trousers, with his hair standing high, shaved up the back. There was a massive smile, a peck on the cheek, and then he led her to his car. Although Nancy lusted for him on sight, being out in public with such an extremely tattooed man was a nervous time. She found herself monitoring people's responses to him, which was generally in the negative, the older the person got. Young people looked, most keeping their expressions neutral, but she could see female admiration as they arrived at the restaurant. She noticed that the valet parkers didn't seem to know him, which was a good thing – at least she wasn't the latest girl to be taken to his favourite place.

The meal was an unimportant blur to Nancy, in which the small talk involved her sister's stay, before the heavy stuff revolved around their lives and plans. She drank a bit more red wine than she normally would. She opened up to him.

Before she knew it, she was at his apartment, on the balcony enjoying the lights of the city. They kissed. He pressed her up against the railing. She giggled at how big he felt down there. She tossed her hair, looked about her, feeling silly because she never giggled. She was cute, adorable, sultry Nancy Niven and she had been with several hunky guys, but this one... this one just blew her mind. She pulled his chest forward to be able to brush her aroused nipples against him. His grin showed his appreciation of the act. His tongue found its way easily into her mouth. He then did two things very well; guided her to his bedroom and removed his top with one muscular swish. Fully tattooed chest, apart from around his left ribcage – left ribcage with iron definition to it. Nancy's long fingers moved over the tattoo patterns, recognising Roman numerals in the centre, Maori work drifting over the left shoulders and a multitude of other stuff, but no loud colours. She reached for his belt as he lowered her to the King-sized bed, but he deflected her attention and was opening her blouse. He seemed to think her belly was the smoothest place he had ever seen in his life so he peppered it with soft kisses. Her hand went to his head. She realised her skirt was undone – when had he done that?

'May I?' he asked.

Oh my God, she thought; nobody had ever asked permission before. *How sweet.*

'Of course,' she replied, after staring into those bright blue eyes.

The skirt disappeared, but without taking her panties with them. His lips were pecking her lower abdomen.

'Perfect skin,' he murmured.

'That's true,' she said, then rolled her eyes and determined to stop waffling like a nervous virgin.

He was up off her. *Oh God, don't move away.* But he was only dimming the lights, and losing his pants on the way back. He returned his attention to her small white panties, playing with the edges, teasing them inwards with his fingertips as if searching for her pubes, then he was kissing her through the fabric. He was grinning, the cheeky man. She was so turned on. The panties were removed in the same action as his top, and Nancy spread her legs for him. He kissed and licked everywhere but on her sex. Forever. Her inner thighs had never had so much attention. It was wonderful. It was expert. It was perfectly timed until he finally opened his mouth and settled down right on her.

6

Jason Ikin was having difficulty keeping his Honda Civic on the twisting roads of darkest Bedfordshire. It was not a case of drink or drugs impeding his driving, nor of bad weather conditions. In fact, it was a lovely, clear night with a fabulous panorama of stars right across the sky. He accelerated hard, and again glanced in the rear view mirror for any sign of the police. The driving problem was not even down to his slightly torn hamstring from a recent rugby game, or the fact that he had been punched by an irate man-mountain on the opposition team, who seemed to want to beat him to death. It was all down to the bare arse he was spanking with his left hand, the passenger seat flat and his fairly willing victim with her skirt and panties around her ankles and letting out little squeals of pain with every blow. Enjoying himself, Jason gave an involuntary laugh before correcting the steering again, then glanced across as she was turning back over. Immediately, he used his hand more gallantly until there came the sounds of orgasm in the darkened cabin.

'Turn back over,' he said urgently to his girlfriend.

'Sod off,' replied Annie Dyer. 'It bloody well hurts.'

'Oh, go on, pleeease.'

She huffed. 'Okay. Once more, only.'

Annie turned over onto her front to have her stinging bottom fondled by her boyfriend. He had a look at her gorgeous rear, with the street lights flickering over the fabulous thing. When the Honda was on a straight stretch of road, he resumed his spanking, really giving it to her, left, right, left, right, only stopping as they came to traffic lights. Annie didn't know it, of course, but he stopped deliberately alongside an articulated lorry, instead of behind it. And Jason didn't know it, of course, but maybe the lorry driver looked down on the semi-naked woman in the compromising position. Maybe.

They set off again. Jason's arm started to ache with the repetition of slapping at an odd angle, giving it some to the back of the legs, too, and getting between the cheeks when she lifted up.

Further into the journey, Annie called a definitive halt to the fun and games and set about fixing her clothing and her seating. She was huffing and blowing at the experience.

'I'm hungry,' she announced, flopping down into position and doing up her belt, before putting the interior light on and checking her appearance in the sun visor mirror. Satisfied, she banged it back up and returned them to darkness.

'Hungry?' asked Jason, incredulous. 'What, again?'

'Yes, again. Where are we, anyway?'

'In the middle of bleedin' nowhere.'

'But, babeeee, I'm hungry again.'

'There's a *Snickers* bar in the glove compartment. You can have that.'

'What a gentleman you are,' she replied, with heavy sarcasm.

She decided to ignore the chocolate bar. They drove on in silence for a while. It allowed Jason to think back to the previous day's rugby game. They had won it 23-21, but it had almost been abandoned after a brawl sprang up, following a high tackle on Dan. Punches had been thrown, throats grabbed, referee and linesman trampled in the melee. Jason had tried to act as peacemaker, a little too soon for one member of the other team who hit him with a haymaker right hand on the left cheekbone, knocking him spark out.

Jason's stomach rumbled. All the effort of driving out to the sticks for that restaurant had burned off the calories. But smacking Annie's bottom had been great fun. She had the best bum he had known for a long time. He grinned in the darkness.

'Tell me, then,' said Annie.

'Tell you what?'

'What your best mate Tony said on the phone, earlier. Was it about this year's rugby tour, by any chance?'

'Errr, yes, babe, it was about that.'

'Is it going to interfere with our holiday plans?'

'Ah, now, it might just do that, babe.'

She sulked for a little while. 'Where is it, then, this year?'

'Romania.'

'Rofuckingmania!? Romania!? As in fucking Dracula Romania? Jesus, Jason.' She folded her arms and looked out at fleeting shadows. 'Well, God, okay, I suppose. Though it's nearly in fucking Asia.'

She shuffled on her seat, her bottom feeling quite abused. She loved it like that, really. She loved Jason, resting her hand on his thigh. '*Hungry*, baby.'

'Would you like me to pull over and kill a cow for you?'

'Don't be sarcastic. So, we're a long way from civilisation?'

'A long way. You are the one who chose that particular country pub.'

'A really long way?'

'Yes.'

She reached for the button fly of his jeans. He did a comedy double-take down there. A grin spread across his bruised face.

7

Gail Hoffman, an eighteen-year-old girl from the city of Renton, just outside Seattle, sipped from her bottle of Evian water while listening to the Assistant Director screaming at someone through the walkie talkie on her hip. Actually screaming. That nice Englishman. At least he wasn't shouting at her, she thought. To be fair, her first ever job as a Production Assistant, or Runner, was going brilliantly well. She was loving it to death. Everyone had been helpful, the Actors and the Extras proving to be polite and accommodating. Perhaps the only negative was the inclement weather out on location, somewhere in Northern California, so she pulled her Seahawks hat down further and snuggled into her North Face fleece. It was a shame after spending so much time doing her hair and perfecting her clothes for the assignment – light green camo trousers, which said she wasn't afraid to get stuck in, but also that she had a great ass, and a white shirt that exposed her flat abdomen. She was working hard and being very conscientious, but she also hoped to find a new boyfriend through this new work. A cameraman or a stuntman, perhaps.

It had been exciting, that morning, to be instructed to collect five male Extras in the VW van, and the handsome guys had all flirted with her, but the rain and cold had dampened their ardour, and a six hour wait had turned them into sullen, shuffling hulks.

She watched them, sheltering in a farmer's barn, near to where the film set had been constructed, all in their coats, and two with their hoods up, some drinking foul catering coffee, one texting his agent with a complaint, no doubt. She checked their names again on her clipboard, just in case any of them were called for individually; Justin, Ryan, Henry (with the full beard), Jake and Tom, all mid-twenties, all picked from their agency for their firm, six-foot physiques, to play soldiers. Gail grinned, looking at their bare lower legs, all fairly camp in Roman sandals. Before the coats were zipped up tight she had seen their Legionnaire tunics and muscular thighs, all self conscious to be without trousers. It took an hour at the farm before they stopped joking with each other over the dresses they were wearing and relaxed into them. Gail had watched the men talk about everything from their girlfriends' problems to their favourite baseball teams, seeing their mannerisms – a subconscious scratch of the balls from one, a spit from another, some bad language, and one taking a pee against a tree. That had been Jake. The lady in the Make-Up department had needed to cover up a set of numbers on his neck, 21-9-2015, which were a tattoo celebrating the birth of his first son. Gail had been fascinated watching that done in a Winnebago back at base, as well as watching Tom try to get used to his new e-cigarette after recently quitting smoking, and Ryan having a good stretch after getting out of the van. Not forgetting Henry pulling the legs of his Boxer shorts down his thighs to attain comfort.

Her radio crackled. Lost in her lustful reverie, she didn't realise at first it was for her.

'Gail!'

'Gail here. Go ahead.'

'Bring the Roman soldiers on to set, please. ASAP.'

'Will do!'

The rain had stopped, but all the men stepped into their Wellington boots to squelch through the mud, following after Gail. They came through a small wood to be met by a bustling film set of lights and cameras, all protected from the weather, and a film crew getting on with things, despite their own misery. The set was a Roman bathhouse and stable block. Bedraggled slaves lingered about. The main actors for the scene were there, talking to the Director. Gail held her group back. She looked at the track for the camera dolly which circled the set, and she knew that the main actors were arriving after a battle to soak their battered bodies. Clearly the Director wanted to make best use of the magnificent bathhouse, intending to pan right around it as the actors arrived on horseback, then follow them inside, where her guys were to already be.

The Assistant Director approached Gail. He looked about twelve but he seemed extremely competent to her, and came with a good reputation back in his native England. Although he had been the man shouting earlier, he gave her a warm smile. 'Gail. It's bloody awful weather. Would you be so kind as to put your people inside? On action, tell them to let the slave girls undress them, and to only get in the water if they don't hear cut. Important, yes, darling? Don't get them all wet unless we are following through on the shot.'

'Yes, sir. Got that.'

'Good. You're an absolute darling.'

Gail turned to her charges. They were nodding, all clear on what was required of them. A brilliant smile appeared through Henry's beard, and Ryan winked at her. In they trudged, leaving their boots out of camera shot. Jake was clapping his hands on his arms.

'At least the water's hot,' pointed out Ryan.

'And the slave girls,' said Henry.

One of the scantily-clad slave girls grinned at them. It was not a porn movie, but was trying to be authentic and explicit.

'First positions!' called somebody.

The actors mounted their horses and rode off out of shot. Then the rain came again, causing a great deal of vile swearing, but the Director needed to get something in the can.

'Let's try for it!' called the Director. He looked at his Cameraman, 'Ready, William?' A hooded form sitting beside the camera nodded at him. 'Action!!'

Gail watched through a window from a distance as her men started to undress, with nubile slave girls assisting with their uniforms. But the actors didn't move, the Director's instructions lost in the downpour. Runners had to wave frantically to let the actors know it was time to go.

'Cut!' screamed the Director. 'Let's go again. Harrison, get closer to the horses and watch me.' A minion trotted off into position.

On the second Action the actors spurred their horses into shot, but Gail's men had missed the call and were still re-dressing and flirting with the slaves. The Director swore foully. The Assistant Director rushed to Gail's side.

'Gail,' he shouted inside the hood of her coat. 'Get inside there, out of sight. I'll double click the walkie-talkie and you say action to your people.'

'Yes, sir!'

Gail ran into the bathhouse, to be greeted with cheers by the men.

'Hush, you guys,' she said, squatting down out of sight. The rain hammered on the plywood roof. It was hot in there with the steaming bath. Her men were oozing sex appeal in the tight space. Gail was quite overawed. 'Listen to me for the action signal. Okay?'

Justin was trying to get a slave girl's number. Jake had wiped off the make-up on his arm and was explaining the significance of the tattoo to another girl. Gail sulked a little, jealous of the raven-haired models flirting with her men. She threw off her hood, tossed her hair a little. Then she reminded herself enough to concentrate, to listen to the radio.

The two clicks came suddenly and she gave the instruction to start. Then, from her position near the floor, Gail watched as all the soldiers were slowly undressed. Gentle female hands assisted with the removal of garments. Everybody was trying not to grin. The "dresses" came down, revealing firm buttocks, hard ribcages and strong manly legs. Only Henry let the side down by having to quickly drop his illicit Boxer shorts, but he was at the back and she was relieved not to be in trouble for that. Her eyes were like saucers. She was all agog. Six naked hunks in front of her. Ryan decided to take his sandals off, so sat right next to her, his solid, slightly hairy, abdomen folding at his hip as he bent forward, his wispy pubes at her eye level, the start of his massive cock going down to be hidden by his thigh. The other men were going into the water with their footwear on. It was Jake who happened to turn sideways first, allowing Gail a full eye-level view of his magnificent manhood. It was so thick, and his balls were hairless. Gail didn't blink. She seemed to have been forgotten down there. She was squatting amid an orgy of testosterone. Good God, she thought, as Henry cupped his scrotum protectively before stepping down into the hot bath, giggling at the temperature.

Then the actors entered the scene, talking and demonstrating sword movements to each other, as other slave girls rushed to deal with them. Ryan stood, with his ass so close to Gail's face that she could see goosebumps on his bare cheeks. She gasped. Justin went into the water with a splash. Then a nude Tom spotted her down there. He winked, grinned, and took his impossible six-pack into the water. Gail thought, if she worked in film and television for forty years, it would never get any better than her first job.

8

'Yes, Chef!'

Lunchtime service was well underway at the best Indonesian restaurant in Bethnal Green, East London. It was a hot day in the capital, so litres of water were being drunk by the sweating chefs, with Simon from New South Wales having to change the bandanna round his blond dreadlocks, and the normally pale Neil, from Dublin, looking like he was having a coronary.

'Two Roti Prata, two Bandeng Presto!'

'Yes, Chef!'

'Yes, Chef!'

Head Chef, Aldi, who came from Surabaya in Indonesia, took several used pans over to the dish wash station, finding his Kitchen Porter only just arriving for work, 'Late again, Eddi?'

'Sorry, Chef.'

Aldi turned, wiped his face and monitored what new chef, Nigel, was up to, which was quite worrying, actually, and would need another one-to-one lesson. Then he went back to Eddi. 'It's tonight, isn't it!?'

Eddi, a handsome Indonesian man, despite his full-length rubber apron and John McEnroe sweatband hiding his eyebrows, beamed his delight that Chef had remembered. 'Yes, Chef!'

'I'll be sure to watch.'

Reza, Aldi's number two, also from Surabaya, asked, 'Watch what, Chef?'

'Eddi's sister is on *Britain's Got Talent* tonight.'

Reza was thrilled. 'Is she!? Doing what?'

'She's a singer,' called Eddi.

'So at least someone in the family has got some talent.'

Eddi offered his friend two fingers, 'Are these yours?'

'*Britain's Got Talent*?' called Neil, in his strong Irish brogue. 'Jesus fucking Christ, the audience scream and applaud all the way through every fucking song. Do me a favour! I don't watch it, never will.' That out of his system, Neil wound up his sleeves, revealing an impressive Shamrock tattoo on his right forearm, and got back to work.

A new check came in from a waitress, which Aldi accepted and shouted it out.

'Yes, Chef!' came from Ding, their Chinese member of staff. Ding had a cute, round face and permanent smile which made him popular with the waitresses. He grinned at Reza. 'Hey, Reza, is it true you applied for *MasterChef* and the BBC turned you down?'

'Ha-ha, very funny,' answered Reza.

'How can it be *Britain's Got Talent*, anyway, when half the acts are foreigners?' asked Simon.

Aldi nodded firmly at that.

Simon leant on his work station while drinking water from a bottle, watching one of the English waitresses as she went into a fridge. She had a bouncy ponytail and very white skin, like a doll, above her black blouse. She grinned at the handsome Aussie – they had slept together once recently and she was hoping to get a repeat performance soon. It was lovemaking to her, and a bang to him.

'Hello, Simon,' she purred.

'Melissa. Looking good, sweetheart.'

'Thank you.'

She wiggled her hips on her way back out front.

'What did I watch last night?' asked Reza. 'Oh, yes, it was about people training to be London bus drivers. All of them were bloody foreign. From like Ghana and places. So, immigrants driving buses full of immigrants.'

'That's London for you,' stated Aldi.

More checks came in. The chefs got busy. For all their moaning about heat and pressure, they could not live without it. Aldi told off a waitress for checking Facebook on her phone, then looked across at the pot wash station where Eddi was working frantically amid the steam. 'Eddi, where's your sidekick, Gary?'

'Gary rang in sick, Chef.'

'What's wrong with him?'

'He said he was shot in the war and his leg is hurting him.'

Aldi stared at Eddi, speechless.

'What war would that be?'

'I guess the Second Gulf War, Chef.'

'Fucking hell. I've heard it all now.'

It was summer in the ski resort of Madesimo, in Italy, close to the Swiss border, north of Milan. Hot weather and the occasional little pillow of cloud, high in the clear blue. Quite a beautiful part of the world. The four Mazza brothers, all in their late twenties, all well-built, all with fairly long dark hair, were gathered to do maintenance work on their mother's little B&B hotel in the town centre. All the brothers worked as either ski instructors or ski shop managers during the season, then did various things to earn money the rest of the year. It was always a boisterous affair whenever the boys got together, shouting playful abuse at each other and making crude jokes. Nino and Francesco were high up on ladders from the side patio, repairing some guttering, while Andrea and Paolo were painting window frames from inside the first floor. There was plenty of chatter with the neighbours and anyone passing who they happened to know. Pretty women were wolf whistled as a matter of routine.

Francesco wanted to talk about Internazionale soccer team but he was shouted down by his AC Milano fanatic brothers, prompting an exchange of virulent hand gestures. So they talked about what friends were doing, about matters regarding the town, and about what Mama was doing for lunch. Andrea was so ready for his lunch, sitting himself down on the window ledge to look at the view of the mountain. His Mama made wonderful pasta, and she would be shouting them very soon, surely. Come on, Mama!

Somebody was shouting, but it wasn't their Mama. Andrea leant out and looked up, but his brothers were silent in their work, starting to look about themselves for the source of the disturbance. Looking down, Andrea saw the bright white blouse and denim skirt of a pretty young woman, shading her eyes from the sun.

'Paolo!' she now screamed. 'Paolo! You little fuck!'

On the first floor, Paolo exchanged a puzzled look with Andrea before looking over the ledge.

'You fuck!' screamed the dark-haired beauty.

'Claudia!? What's wrong with you?'

'You went with my sister, you bastard!'

'What!? Don't be ridiculous.'

'Come down! I'm going to cut your fucking balls off!'

'Now, now, Claudia...'

Paolo's brothers were screaming with laughter. Francesco told him to go down and face the music. Nino called his kid brother a coward, and almost fell off his ladder, so amused was he.

'Paolo, have you been a bad boy?' teased Nino.

'Claudia...' pleaded Paolo.

'Don't Claudia me, you son of a bitch!'

'Claudia...'

Mama Mazza came into view, to see what all the noise was. She put her arms around the distraught teenager, then gesticulated rudely up at her sons indiscriminately, knowing what they were all like, before taking the girl inside.

'Oh, shit,' said Paolo, rushing inside.

Andrea frowned, worried that this would delay his lunch. He followed Paolo, to monitor the situation. Francesco and Nino got themselves up onto the roof and rested for a while. Their shirts came off. Francesco, the eldest, shook his hair from his eyes and squinted at the sun. Then he asked his brother what his plans were for the summer. Nino gestured vaguely, then traced the line of sweat down the middle of his chest.

'Why don't you go back to Uncle Gianni's restaurant in London?' Francesco asked. 'You liked it there. You had that sweet girl there.'

Nino shrugged. He let his mind wander back to the nice Trattoria in Mill Hill, North London. He had more than one sweet girl there. He would chat them up, then take them back to the rented house which ten members of staff shared, and screw them until the sun came up.

These two brothers were the ski instructors in the family, which was much easier than slogging their guts out in the ski shop, six days a week. Nino would prefer to spend his summer socialising with his friends or working on his old Alfa Romeo. Francesco was just out of a two year relationship with a girl from Milan, so he would prefer to have a work-free summer, recharge his emotional batteries. Basically, all the Mazza brothers wished they were wealthy playboys. More raised voices came up to them from the kitchen.

'Paolo. Paolo,' bemoaned Francesco.

The two brothers laughed, then lay back to enjoy the sun.

9

The former hospital resembled a Gothic monastery, sitting on a mound near to the M1 motorway, not far from Watford, in Hertfordshire. During the First World War it had served as a convalescence home for wounded soldiers. Since its closure in 2002 it had appeared in one of those Most Haunted television documentaries on Sky, and been home to two hundred Gypsy families. Grade 2 listed, about to be developed into luxury apartments, it was being used by a pharmaceuticals firm for its latest drug trial.

There were eight men on the trial on one particular wing seven were on the experimental liver drug and one was on the placebo. Obviously, and smugly, the man on the placebo was 24-year-old Martin, as he was the only resident in the dormitory not to have turned yellow. He knew he was earning his £1000 cheque without taking any risks, without his head swelling or his organs failing. Martin lounged on his bed, enjoyed his meals, played pool and read his Playstation and Xbox magazines. His only inconvenience was the catheter in his left arm (which all the men had) from which blood was taken three times a day. Martin was also the only man not to have raging flatulence. The hospital reeked, men breaking wind every other minute, to the point that it had become hilarious. Family had been allowed to visit halfway through the four week trial and they found it hard to believe the funk they walked into to which smell the men had clearly become immune.

Despite all that, the eight were enjoying great camaraderie. They had film nights, played cards, laughed and joked. They were a mixed bunch: contented Martin in Bed One; in Two was Naseem, a thirty-year-old family man who was a self-employed market trader. Robert was in Three, a professional drug trialist who travelled the country taking whatever was given to him, as long as the fee was worth it. Tommy occupied Bed Four. He was a good-looking Graphic Designer, there because business was slow, and his friend Martin had talked him into it. Tommy liked to work out, and was allowed to by the nurses, as long as he protected his catheter. On one of the good weather days they had actually played a game of football on the car-park. Tommy was also the joker, crude at times, keeping morale up, as well as the organiser who set times for when they did things together. In Five was Andy, a builder, there also because of financial worries. He worked out with Tommy, and spent his entire time there wearing only shorts and Reebok mules. Two of the nurses had rated the fuckability of Tommy and Andy, and the occupant of Bed Six was also popular. Andy had been the most concerned about them turning yellow, but believed the doctors when they assured him it was a temporary development. So he worked on his yellow six-pack, won the pool competition and texted his girlfriend non-stop. Taking up Bed Six was another hunk, twenty-eight-year-old Carl, a car salesman, who just wanted some quick, easy cash to pay for a holiday in Magaluf. Carl was the reader of the group, having got through *Shogun*, and still involved with *Bhowani Junction* and *Sexting*, depending on his mood. Beds Seven and Eight had two friends from medical school, Benjamin and Hugh. Naturally, the pharmaceutical firms targeted medical students, who carried a lot of personal debt and were more aware of the trials anyway. Both of the boys, in their early twenties, were studious and quite posh, but they took part in the banter as loudly as the next man.

Carl let rip with a massive fart which raised a cheer. Nurse Caroline happened to be on the ward. She said, through pursed lips, 'Dear me. Dear me. I wasn't born for this,' and went on her way, followed by bawdy laughter.

Tommy was assessing his catheter, still horrified by the memory of the nurse digging away manically in search of a vein. 'I'm sure that fucking bitch has damaged my vein. I'm all bruised under the skin.'

'Christ, I need a shag!' suddenly came from Andy. 'It's getting to me now.'

'Ask Nurse Holly,' suggested Martin. 'She'll sort you out.'

'Right now I'd bang Nurse Rachel,' said Andy, prompting much hilarity, as Rachel was in her sixties and very strict with them on the night shift.

Tommy broke wind satisfactorily. 'Just tug one off, like Benjamin, over there.'

'Hey!' objected Benjamin, laughing. 'Hey. That's a bit harsh. All right? Harsh. Harsh but true.'

'Shall we have a darts competition tonight, boys?' asked Tommy.

'Oh, yes,' shouted Hugh.

'Well, what do we have here?' asked Tommy. 'Our boy Hugh sounded so keen he must be a ringer. Have you had a One Hundred and Eighty, Hugh, you devious little fucker?'

'Several times, actually.'

'We won't play for money, then.'

Hugh laughed. Then expelled the greatest amount of gas so far, causing uproar. Naseem almost went into hysterics.

Doctor Barnes entered the dorm, not even pretending to hide his horror at the smell. 'Shit! Everyone feeling all right?'

When everybody answered in the affirmative, the Doctor turned on his heels and departed. Martin jumped up and headed to the verandah to continue his sunbathing. Hugh and Benjamin decided to shoot some pool. Everyone else lay on their beds, with a long afternoon ahead of them before tea.

'I spy...' said Robert, after a moment.

The following morning, after blood had been taken, Doctor Barnes had made his flying visit, with his catchphrase, 'Shit! Everyone feeling all right?' Then breakfast had been consumed. Tommy decided to go for a shower. It was a glorious day, temperature-wise, and the shower felt wonderful, apart from knocking his catheter a couple of times and swearing obscenely. Despite farting like a trooper, Tommy looked at his buff body in the mirror and felt pleased that his skin seemed to be losing its yellow tinge. He headed back into the dorm and stood there in just his towel until he had everyone's full attention.

'I've seen some sights in my time but that is fucking horrible!' Tommy recounted his first meeting with a new nurse that morning. 'I walked through a door into her. I nearly died of shock. Fuck me, I thought, that's rough. It shouldn't be allowed out in public.' The other men were laughing hysterically at him. He was being so serious and intense over it. 'Dreadful, lads. Dreadful. Absolutely fucking awful, I tell you.' More screams of hilarity. Tommy crossed his arms. 'I'll say it again...' He broke off to laugh himself. 'I've seen some sights in my time but that is fucking horrible.' Right on cue, a very large, extremely unattractive nurse entered the dorm behind Tommy. Naseem disappeared under his bed sheets, Carl tried to gesture Tommy to be quiet. 'Fucking terrible. It should have been put down at birth...'

10

In the thirty-six hours since the four Americans had ridden their motorbikes off the ferry from Liverpool at the back of a mass of riders, the excitement had not diminished. If anything, it had increased. One of the men rode a Ducati Monster 1200, another a Suzuki Hyabusa, and the two others were on Honda Fireblades. After five years of planning, juggling work schedules, postponing a marriage, the four friends were finally on the Isle of Man, in the middle of the Irish Sea. It was TT week, or Tourist Trophy, the world famous motorcycle races through the towns and over the mountain – the totally un-politically correct craziness that could be found nowhere else in world sport.

Michael was the leading figure in arranging the trip. A twenty-seven-year-old model, currently residing in Miami, he was obsessed with the sheer insanity of the races, with the risks, the crashes, the absolute guts of the riders who took part. From the first time he watched YouTube footage through a bike's visor as it hurtled past stone walls on closed public roads at over 130 mph, he had been obsessed with the race. It really was death-defying and the men who took part were superhuman in Michael's eyes.

The four were camping on an official site a couple of miles outside of Douglas, the island's capital. There were parties going on, barbecues, new friendships being made, mutual appreciation of each other's bikes, superstar riders to see and try to attain autographs from, practice sessions to go and watch, and then the first of the races.

Joe, the owner of the red Hyabusa, which garnered the most attention, was a college buddy of Michael. He was a dentist from Charleston, whose wife had allowed him to come, and he was deliriously happy, given that he had Irish roots and knew ancestors had moved to Liverpool in the 1860's. After the TT, they were spending a couple of days in Dublin, before flying back to the States.

Steven was the one who had postponed his marriage, to the adorable Bethany, back home in Sarasota, Florida. She knew how long he had wanted this. She was a darling. He texted her constantly from their tent. Their latest communication: '*I love you, baby. Have a great time there. You can make love to me all night when you get back.*'

'*All night?*'

'*Can you not manage it? Hehe.*'

'*Got to go. I love you.*'

'*I love you.*'

'I love you more, Babyboo.'

Dan, the fourth member of the group, kicked Steven's leg. It was time to go. Dan laughed and pulled Steven to his feet. Dan was Michael's cousin, and hailed from New Jersey. Even in his bike leathers, Dan had that sexy v-shape body, and with a crew-cut he was the most handsome of all the men. He smiled at Michael. Today was Mad Sunday. Today the general public were allowed to ride the course. Dan and Michael high-fived, laughing. Steven put his phone away, smiled and let himself be pulled into a hug. Joe, still tugging himself into his leathers, hopped over to join in.

So, with great joy, they rode slowly out of the camp, going with the flow of other bikes, as well as cars. Hundreds of bikes, in fact. All moving slowly behind a marshall's vehicle before they negotiated the town boundaries, and then, once out into the countryside, they could flow freely. The four Americans were not being crazy, not trying to stay with the bikes who flew off at great speed, but they were going to enjoy themselves. They got by three cars before opening up, with Michael in the lead on his Ducati machine, then Dan, Steven, Joe. Other bikes overtook them. Immediately, they saw a rider and his bike down in a field, with his friends stopped at intervals along the road. It seemed a minor incident. On they rode, twisting and turning, low walls everywhere. The road started to rise. Michael led them around a Ford Mondeo, then they overtook two bikes with girl pillion passengers. All the time faster bikes were flying by them. Michael built up the speed. He decided to stay behind a group of bikes, to be led along. It was intensely exhilarating. Everyone overtook two cars in turn, then they were up on the mountain, a blur of green flashing by. Michael looked back at his friends. He was loving it. This was a dream come true. He gave them a fist pump. Then he took the bend, straightened and looked back, seeing Dan come round, then Steven, then Joe appeared. But Joe failed to take the bend, went straight into a low stone wall, which catapulted him head first like a rag doll into the field beyond.

'Those tits are fucking amazing.'

One of the three men said it, but all were thinking it. Tits were, somewhat, the men's business. They saw them every day. They filmed them, they thought up ways to make them bounce around, they advised when they were too small and in need of enhancement. But they were watching Kendall Hawthorne (not her real name) and her natural, firm, very pointed breasts needed no surgery. Kendall's skin was fair, smooth and beyond compare. Blonde, twenty-six, a wide, sexy mouth which could smile easily if she had a nicer personality. Her hips were wide, at that precise moment having her black thong rearranged along them. Perhaps her legs were too thin, bent at the knees as she knelt on the white bed.

'Thirty seconds, Kendall,' said the man who had voiced their thoughts.

He threw a cell phone onto the bed. His name was Fran. Beside him stood Ian. Both men were producers on this late-night arse-wiggling show beaming out to the Great British public from a

Hounslow warehouse. There were three beds partitioned off, a bathroom set and a BDSM dungeon, although everything was quite tame. Cindy (not her real name) was in the bath, pouting and playing with the soap. Alice (her real name because she didn't give a monkey's) was in the chains and leather g-string, simulating being taken roughly from behind. Her partner for the evening, Jessica (not her real name, real tits or real hair) was currently on her break. The two beds either side of Kendall contained Phoenix Marie (self explanatory) spanking herself, and Lulu Jade (ditto) who was the only one actually talking to a paying punter on her phone, while fondling her 34DD boobs through a pink bra.

Kendall tossed her hair. The third man watching her was Oddie (only Administration knew his real name) who gave her the thumbs up from behind his camera. Kendall's shift started, so she gave her best sexy look into the lens, bouncing slightly, waggling the phone to encourage a call.

'Looking great, Kendall, darling,' said Ian, as there was no sound on the show, just the same music pumped across all five channels.

Kendall smiled at him, and he felt honoured, then she dropped the phone and pulled both breasts out by the nipples.

Oddie knew some of his fellow cameramen were jaded and bored with the work, but he still loved coming in every night. He was thirty-three, starting to lose his looks, but he had been with a few of the models. He still appreciated beauty, especially Kendall. He watched her get onto her hands and knees to simulate going down on a man. Her rear was extraordinarily sexy, the thong tight between her cheeks. Her back was sleek. He could see both of her conical breasts hanging down. She pulled her hair away from the camera, revealing a thin neck. Then she eyed the camera as her head bobbed frantically. Oddie got comfortable on his seat, looking forward to Kendall's full repertoire, which usually included ankles behind the head at some stage.

Fran, a muscly Irishman, who had started out promoting illegal cage fighting, then done well in tele-sales before stumbling into pornography, was the only one of the three to have been with Kendall. When she came in to work he always allowed himself a brief reminisce of their torrid six month affair, starting with the wild sex and finishing with the insane arguing, and then he would be professional and polite with her.

Ian, although he had dated one model, was more of a gentleman. He was successful in a number of television projects, and only came into the warehouse two or three times a week. He was a big man, too, although he wouldn't want to mess with Fran. He enjoyed Kendall spanking herself red as she spoke to her first caller. Then he turned to Fran and suggested they order in a takeaway. Fran gave a nod, slapped Oddie on the back, and the two producers went up to the Control Room to put their feet up and eat heartily while the money rolled in.

11

Leo Rooney was open and honest with Nancy, in that he was busy with building up his photographic studio in Harlem, not to mention his imminent home move. So there was to be no rushing into any kind of relationship. Not that Nancy was sure she wanted that, anyway. She was suddenly tired and stressed from everything that had gone on recently. This vacation, which Daniel was still keen for her to take, was becoming more and more tempting by the minute.

She enjoyed the remainder of her sister's stay, before seeing Lucy off at the airport in a big emotional scene, promising to come home soon. She then spent a couple of days tidying up loose ends in the office and, over a working brunch with Zach, he announced his own plan to go home to North Carolina for a week or two.

'Zach, my adorable Zachy, I'll miss you so much.'

His expression was dead-pan. 'No, you won't.'

'Meh, true. How's George?'

George was Zach's boyfriend. The three of them had spent a wonderful day recently, hitting baseballs from inside batting cages, a total, unmitigated sporting failure for Nancy, followed by hot dogs and beer. Nancy had known a few gay people back home in England (even had a brief lesbian thing herself while at Uni) but nothing compared to the perfection that was Zach and George: two human beings so in love and just perfect for each other.

'He's well,' Zach told her. 'He can't wait to see my folks again. I swear, he loves my mother more than he does me.'

'Now, that's impossible and you know it, Zachy.'

Zach grinned at her.

'Are you two getting married?' asked Nancy.

'Oh, there's an idea.'

So, all systems go – time to buy a couple of new bikinis, sun cream and sunglasses, and whatever else she could think of. That meant a shopping trip with friend, Gabby, who showed jealousy at the skimpy outfits Nancy's nubile body could carry off so easily. At lunch afterwards, Gabby expressed fascination in the location for Nancy's trip. What would it be like to work for a firm with its own, private little Caribbean island?

'It's so like *The Thorn Birds*,' said Gabby, between bites.

'How is it like *The Thorn Birds*?'

'Well, Meggie goes off to that island to be alone, if I remember properly. Then Father Ralph shows up. And... hehem. So, where exactly are you going?'

'I'm not too sure. Private jet, then helicopter. I think there are a few villas on the island. It's all very exclusive.'

'But, Nancy, you're going alone? Will you be safe?'

'That's something I did ask about. A security firm covers several islands and they come if you call on the radio. But I'll be fine. No riff-raff can get out there.'

Gabby laughed. 'Well, I hope you have a lovely rest. You've had a crazy year.'

'Thank you, Gabby. I wish you could come with me.'

'So do I, but I'll be in the Hamptons. A working, put-upon nanny, but in the Hamptons.'

Twenty minutes later, when Gabby turned down coffee, Nancy asked for and paid the bill. At the next table, a smartly-dressed woman with too much gold jewellery stood to greet the arrival of a girlfriend, who was equally well-attired, with sunglasses on her head and a Burberry bag on her left wrist. They carried out very pretentious and loud air kisses, which got Nancy and Gabby's full attention.

'Xenobia, darling,' said the first woman, as they seated themselves. 'It's lovely to see you. We really, really must do this more often.'

'And it's lovely to see you, Tiff. Yes, we absolutely must.'

They ordered wine from the waiter.

'Tiffany, don't you look astonishing. You're such a gym-bunny.'

Gym-bunny? mimed Nancy at Gabby.

'I've heard you've got a new boyfriend,' said Tiffany.

'How on earth did you hear? Dear me, he's my secret.' She giggled. 'Oh, darling, he's gorgeous. But we're having a little trouble communicating because he doesn't speak English and I don't speak Spanish.'

Nancy and Gabby held it in until they were outside the restaurant, then burst into laughter and fell into each other. Gabby had the honour, 'He doesn't speak English and I don't speak Spanish.' And they screamed with laughter again.

The two friends went home to Nancy's apartment for a cup of Yorkshire tea and some Eccles cakes, brought by Lucy from England. On the sofa, with the panoramic view of nothing very inspiring spread out before them, Nancy finally told Gabby about Leo, a topic which had been eating away at her. She was reluctant to share him in any way. He was just too good to be true – so confident in who he was that he could cover himself in all that multi-coloured ink.

'And you're leaving the country?' asked Gabby, astounded. 'Take your vacation in his bed, you stupid girl.'

'He's busy with his career.'

'Nonsense. Look at you, woman. Gorgeous. Flit those black Indonesian eyes at him. Tattooed, you say, up under his chin? How extraordinary. And a photographer? I demand to meet him.'

'Patience, will you, please? Gabby, I don't want to be too forward with him, you know. And, besides, I am a bit frazzled. Two weeks of beautiful solitude ahead of me. Peace and quiet and a fully stocked kitchen. Egyptian cotton sheets, I made that bit up. Re-charge my batteries. Then we'll see where he's at.'

'Where he's at will be in some other girl's bed.'

Nancy frowned. 'Eat your Eccles cake.'

'Okay, you know your own mind. Do you want me to take you to the airport?'

'Thanks, but Daniel is taking me. You know, Daniel, the boss.'

'The boss is taking you to the airport? Oh my God, how do I get a job in this firm? Yes, I've met Daniel, now I recall. Mmmm, he's fit. Oh, bloody hell, Nancy, I think I need to find a new fella.'

'We'll see to it as soon as I get back. I promise.'

Gabby had things to do, so, after dramatic air kisses in honour of Tiffany and Xenobia, Nancy was left alone in her apartment. As she was seeing Leo again before her vacation, she took a shower. He was taking her out, but wouldn't say where, so she dressed sombrely in a dark business suit – not that she ever dressed too sexily in public, being a good, half-Indonesian girl.

He was waiting for her downstairs and, as soon as she saw him grinning at her, she was swooning again and ready to cancel her trip. He was dressed like an English gentleman in a designer green sweater, a matching scarf and a flat cap. He was in black trousers and brown boots. His smile lit up the foyer. He kissed her left cheek, seeming to linger there on her smooth flesh. She let him take her hand.

'So, where are we going?' she asked, smiling up at him. 'Pigeon shooting?'

'You look adorable.'

'Thank you. Where are we going? Is it a secret?'

'I've never felt such a delicate jaw as yours before.'

'Eh?'

As they were moving to go out, Gabby exited the elevator. It was genuinely a coincidence, although she and Nancy shared a grin.

'Oh, you must be the famous Leo?' said Gabby.

Nancy rolled her eyes. '*Gabby.*'

'Oh, hush, you.'

Gabby and Leo shook hands. She was trying to glimpse his ink work around his neck without making it too obvious. Nancy did the official introductions.

'So, you're a photographer, Leo? That is so fascinating. I do love the art of photography.'

'*No, you don't,*' said Nancy.

'Did I not tell you to hush, girl? Anyway, I have to run. It was lovely to meet you, Leo.'

Leo gave her his best smile and they touched hands again, before Gabby skipped out of the building, looking back once.

Leo got the passenger door for Nancy; she slipped in, and watched him jog around to join her.

'Your friend is very nice.' He stared at her for a moment. 'Nancy, you are so, so cute.'

'Thank you, Leo.'

'Do you want to change the music?'

Gus Kaitiff rushed to mind. 'No, no, you're all right. It's fine as it is.' They set off into the traffic. 'So, where are we going?'

'Why do you need to know?'

'I don't, really. What would you like to talk about? How many children you want to have?'

He laughed. 'Nancy, honey, I'm taking you to a snooker game.'

She shot him a sideways glance. 'I beg your pardon? Snooker? As in fifteen reds and all the colours snooker? Snooker loopy snooker?'

'I have no idea what snooker loopy is, but, yes, snooker. It's on at this English pub I go to occasionally. I thought you would like it.'

She thought about watching a game of snooker. An image came to her of snooker on BBC television, her father watching transfixed as a snooker player spent five minutes deliberating over a shot, chalking his cue twenty times, before then playing a simple safety.

'Sounds like fun,' she said.

'Or, if you prefer, an acquaintance of mine is holding an exhibition of watercolour landscape paintings by recently escaped North Korean artists.'

While she was deliberating over the alternative, he started laughing.

'What? Oh, I get it,' she laughed. 'Teasing little me.'

'I'm sorry. Will you forgive me?'

'I'll think about it.'

She realised they were heading into Harlem. Looking out the side window, she had a little smirk to herself; he was taking her to his studio. She needed to forgive him quickly, so ran her left hand up the shaved part of his head, bringing a sideways grin.

The area was busy. Leo was hailed by several friendly people as he led her through the throng. There was one upside-down tennis-style handshake with one man. All eyes were on Nancy. They went up in a glass elevator to a well-lit, airy loft space. The west side was all open to a view of the neighbourhood. The floors were original wood. The brickwork exposed. Straight away, Nancy began to price it up.

Realising she was holding Leo's hand from the elevator, Nancy also instantly began to assess some of his work, hung up or propped against the bottom of walls; of happy people, mainly, but also moody cityscapes, some in colour, quite a lot in black and white. They walked through to where the space began to be partitioned off. She found it all a lovely working environment, with the glass skylights adding to the brightness. In one section they moved amongst portrait art in oil and charcoal. Stunned, she rolled into his arms, giggling.

'Yes, I paint, as well.'

'So, so talented. I... find I like you very much, Mr Rooney.'

They kissed. With tongues. Nancy's eyes sparkled as they came up for air. This could be something really good.

He moved her with romantic shuffling into the next sectioned part of the room, where she was confronted by a fully-laid dining table with candles, napkins and crystal wine glasses.

'I also cook,' he said. 'A going away dinner.'

Nancy almost melted backwards against him.

12

Early morning in New York, Nancy was having toast and her favourite Lampung coffee from Indonesia, as she checked the contents of her suitcase. She was travelling fairly light, with the type of vacation it was in mind; just a shoulder bag and a small Samsonite case containing dresses, jeans, tops, bikinis, underwear, four different sets of shoes. She finished her toast and frowned at the crumbs that would be going with her.

Okay, she was content, sealing the case and getting it to the door. Then she suddenly realised she felt like talking with her mother. She finished her coffee in the kitchen, washed up, then went and jumped onto her sofa, grabbing the phone to call England. She made the home phone in London ring out three times before hanging up, which was the signal for her technophobe Mum to find her Kindle and stumble onto Skype. Nancy picked up her own tablet and, after waiting a couple of minutes, tried to get through. Usually she failed time and time again, or just got sound, but this time she heard all the right noises and then the 1970's swirls of her parents' lounge ceiling popped up on the screen.

'Mummy? Are you there?'

Her mother's pixilated face appeared, smiling. 'Darling, can you hear me? I can't see you. Oh, right, I must press that button, now I remember. Ah, there you are, my baby. But I thought you were away on holiday.'

'I'm going soon, Mummy. I just wanted to see you first.'

'Nancy, you've come through in the middle of *Bargain Hunt*.' The Kindle panned round to the BBC antiques show on the television, where "experts" helped two teams try to find bargains at car-boot sales to sell at auction. 'Look, my favourite, Mark Stacey, is on today.'

'It's probably a repeat, Mummy. Are you well? How's Daddy?'

'We're both fine, darling. How are you?'

The Kindle remained facing the television so Nancy watched *Bargain Hunt* for the entire twenty minute chat with her mother. The story she had told her mother was that she and Gabby were going away together on a glamping trip to New Hampshire – no need to worry the woman unnecessarily with tales of Robinson Crusoe.

After the Skype call, Nancy felt better. At least everything was fine at home. She looked around her apartment. She checked everything was turned off in the kitchen and the window blinds were down. She put on her favourite Adidas trainers for travelling in and put her hair up in a ponytail. She was good to go. Time to sit and wait for her ride to the airport.

It allowed her to think about the previous night with Leo. The special surprise meal had been an Indian takeout, as it turned out that he could not cook after all, no matter what he had said. But first, with a glass of wine in hand, she had perused all the work in his studio, expressed her liking of certain pictures, and enjoyed the way he held her as he explained the circumstances behind some of the commissions. He then led her up to the roof so they could enjoy the last of the sun and a refreshing breeze. The view filled her with romantic joy, she was in New York City, and firm kissing started to happen, and she managed to get her hands inside his shirt to hold his strong back.

'I will be photographing you,' he had said, breaking off to kiss her left ear.

'You will?' she replied, gasping at the pleasure. 'Okay. Will that be happening tonight?'

He had laughed. 'No, not tonight.'

At the back of the studio there was a small, functional bedroom with en suite bathroom, which Nancy eyed suspiciously, until he explained that he sometimes worked very, very late, and just crashed there. She was accepting that story as he hugged her from behind and began licking her neck. Not kissing, actually licking, upwards, causing her to curl back into him in ecstasy. His hands started on her belly before sliding up to cup her breasts. She was in no rush to turn around, and he was happy to keep her like that, the licking moving around onto her right ear.

'Leo,' she moaned.

He removed her dress in one swift movement, aided by her raised arms. His shirt was gone before she spun to be against his chest, kissing hard with tongues. He had a finger inside her panties, just running inside the hem, yet it drove her crazy with desire. She rushed to get him on the bed, all that hard muscled tattooed chest flopping backwards, with his beaming smile. Nancy knelt in front of him, fiddling with his trousers, pausing once to push hair out of her eyes. She smiled at him. She had his pants open and ordered him to lift up as she tugged them down, making sure not to take his *Superdry* boxers with them. His six-pack rolled up so they could kiss, then she, in all seriousness, pushed him back with the palm of her right hand.

'Stay,' she said. 'Good boy. There's something I've been looking forward to.'

Then, resisting the urge to touch the massive swelling in his shorts, she pulled the material forward to allow him to spring free. Her black Indonesian eyes went wide and she smiled happily. She loved doing that, making the man's erection bounce around. It was beautiful. She took a firm hold on it and poked out her tongue.

13

Daniel Bridgford thought it a bit unfair – alongside him, it was Oliver Hardy doing front kicks into the big red pad held by Stan Laurel, slowly bouncing the smaller, distressed man towards the wall. Not that Daniel was doing much better, with Ulrika being particularly aggressive with her kicks at the pad he was holding. He gave her a "Steady on, girl" expression, which made her smile and back off a little. Or maybe she was tired from her recent globetrotting. Anyway, Big Ronnie called a halt to his Tae Kwon-do lesson, shouted for the pads to be put away and for all his students to join him in cool-down stretches.

'Why no jogging?' Daniel complained to Ulrika in a whisper. 'Why? Why? Why do you get away with the jogging?'

Ulrika just giggled against him.

Ulrika, who was a Blue belt, compared to Daniel's Green, sat beside her boyfriend in her sweaty dobok suit, looking at her man as they both copied Big Ronnie. She had noticed the change in Daniel since returning from Stockholm. Only minuscule, just something a lover would see, but that was enough to suggest he was hiding an illness or an affair. She had questioned him over dinner the previous evening, but he had said he was fine, and again after lovemaking into the early hours. Now, she asked him again, in a soft whisper.

'I'm fine, honey,' he said, brightening from his reverie. 'Just worrying about a work situation. Everything is good, I promise.'

She smiled reassuringly at him. 'Mwah.'

'Mwah.'

It was two airports in one day for Jason Ikin. He dropped girlfriend, Annie, off at her base in Luton Airport, for her Flight Attendant shift to Zurich and back. He really did love her uniform and the little hat with the *Thunderbirds*-style logo she had to wear. He wanted to do her right there and then, somewhere on the premises. She had said something like, "Down, Tiger", pushing him off, but continuing to kiss him. She had forgiven him for going away without her. She understood, and wished him a safe trip. But he was not to do anything even remotely naughty on it. He pulled a face of complete innocence. Then came a lovely, long hug, as neither wanted to be parted for so long. With one more lingering kiss, he let her slip from his fingertips and watched her go inside, with one hip wiggle and a little wave back.

From there, he drove back to their flat to double check his luggage, and be sure that he had his passport (didn't want to make that stupid mistake again). He decided to change his travelling tee-shirt, he liked to show off his biceps but actually hated to be tight under the armpit. This gave him another chance to admire his newly finished shoulder tattoo, completed the previous evening at a shop in Luton town centre. It was a magnificent winged dragon, spitting out a vicious tongue. He couldn't wait to show it off on holiday at every opportunity.

Still, there was a little time for a spot of lunch and to watch an episode of *American Pickers*, his current favourite show, with Frank and Mike looking for antiques in Florida. Then he was on his way to Heathrow – to West Drayton, actually, where he was leaving his car at cousin Simon's place.

After a quick catch-up with Simon, and a promise to bring something back for the missus, he let his cousin lead him up to the bathroom to give him a quote for ripping it out and installing a wet room. Simon seemed happy with the "family rates", they agreed on a provisional date to start work, then Jason declined a drink, as his taxi had arrived. He man-hugged Simon and then he was on his way, and that was when the excitement really hit him. This trip was going to be awesome. He actually took a deep breath, so keyed up was he. He didn't know what to expect, except fun and games, great food, great location: a total new adventure, in fact. Bring it on!

Daniel entered Nancy's apartment, looking tired and unshaven, in ripped jeans and a sweater that made him look like George Clooney in *The Perfect Storm*. Nancy gave him a hug, feeling from his tense chest that he was being standoffish with her.

She nodded when he asked if that was her suitcase. She considered telling him it was a decoy case, but he really seemed distressed about something. Perhaps the reunion with Ulrika had not gone too well, so she held her tongue.

'Are you all set?' he asked.

'Ready for paradise, Boss. My toes crave the wet sand.'

'Good. Good. Let's hope there's no hurricane coming through.'

'No. No hurricane would be a good thing.'

They went down to Daniel's Range Rover, and Nancy hopped in while he loaded her case. Her father owned a similar vehicle, which made her sad for a moment, wanting to go home, run to Daddy's arms, but then she took a deep breath and thought ahead to her amazing Caribbean vacation.

'Thank you so much for doing this, Daniel,' she said, as he started driving.

He didn't say anything. He was really worrying her now. She puzzled over whether to tackle him about it; they had always had an open relationship, not just professional, but then he started to run through her travel details. She had been in the company jet before, when they went to close a deal with a client in Florida, but the helicopter ride from Montego Bay promised to be exciting for her.

'I want you back fresh as a button,' said Daniel, attempting to brighten up. Perhaps he realised that she had noticed his morose state of mind. 'You're one of my best people. Right? Now, are you looking forward to it, seriously?'

'Enoromously.'

'Enoromously? What does that mean?'

She laughed. 'I couldn't say enormous when I was little. It's a joke with my dad. Thank you again for this, Daniel. I am in need of a break. I didn't realise it at first. And this promises to be so memorable.'

'Memorable,' repeated Daniel. 'Yes, it will be memorable. Tell me all about it when you get back. I might go there myself with Ulrika. You just... You be careful out there.'

Congestion on the roads near Heathrow stressed out Jason. He thought about his brother's suggestion to get a new van for the business. He remembered spanking Annie's bottom again. He fretted over Tottenham Hotspurs' summer signings once more. But, finally, he was able to pay off the taxi and lug his bags into Terminal 5. He bought some chewing gum and a Film magazine in a newsagents. As he liked to do when he flew, he people watched for a moment or two, guessing where people were flying to. He bet there weren't many people going where he was.

Then he shouldered his bags. Having flown from there before, he knew his way around Departures. Moving through the crowds, he let his mind drift ahead to the coming adventure. It should be an amazing experience. Somebody barged into him, but he was so happy he apologised, smiled and moved on.

He spotted Darren first, because he was wearing the rugby club colours, then Tony and George were drunkenly hailing him, and he was immediately pulled into a team hug with bouncing and chanting. Airport staff were nearby, watching on with stern expressions. The boys were all here. All eighteen of them, with the Team Coach and the Medic/Kit Man and even the Club Secretary, who liked a jolly outing. Jason immediately took part in the banter. Injuries from the brawl in the last match were compared and laughed about. The boys were here! The boys were on tour!

Romania... lock up your daughters!

14

The helicopter was a very pretty maroon colour, which was about as far as Nancy's interest went with it, and she wished the two boring Canadian pilots up front would give it a rest with the technical talk. She raised her eyebrows in mock interest for the third time, then looked down at the total, gorgeous blue of the Caribbean waters. Take the hint, guys. Shut up and let her enjoy the start of her vacation.

Nancy, of course, was the only passenger. The entire journey from New York had not been too bad but, by that time in the early evening, she just wanted to see the beach, see an alcoholic beverage and see her bed on which to collapse. She was starting to feel silly with the whole solo vacation thing. A rest in an exotic location was all well and good, but there wasn't going to be any Father Ralph de Bricassart showing up.

'Miss Niven,' said the older of the two pilots through her headphones. Wearily, Nancy looked at him. 'We'll be arriving soon. A nice lady called Janet will meet you, help you settle in, show you the radio, deal with any questions, and then she will depart by company speedboat. We trust you'll have a marvellous stay.'

'Thank you so much.'

She started to think that maybe Gabby had been right, that she should have been spending time with Leo. What was he doing right that moment? Bedding a woman who had just posed for him? But then she looked forward between the white shirts and gold epaulettes of the pilots and beheld the lush green island, fringed with a white sand edging. Her heart swelled at the beauty of it, that it was paradise with nothing but blue all around it, and then she felt a burst of adrenalin as an image came to her, that of her being a participant in *I'm A Celebrity, Get Me Out Of Here!* where twelve Z-listers endure a few weeks in the jungle, and where a few of them arrive by parachuting out of a helicopter. But now their machine was descending.

The boring, but clearly competent, older pilot brought the craft in and set them down without even a bump, and then his younger colleague was flinging off his headset to jump out and get Nancy's door. She said thank you again before removing her headset and allowed herself to be assisted out onto the helipad.

The younger pilot guided her to safety before going back to get her luggage. Once that was deposited at her feet, he saluted and ran at a stoop back to the helicopter. While she waited for them to abandon her, Nancy scanned the completely open horizon. She looked at the rocky outcrop where the helipad had been built, then the beautiful white sand curved away before finally ending in lush, green foliage. With a warm breeze on her face and the hot sun beating down, it was close to being that paradise. Not Indonesia, of course, but close.

The helicopter slowly lifted off and headed out to sea. It failed to explode – Nancy berating herself for watching too many action films recently. Then domestic practicalities kicked in, wondering where the hell this Janet woman was, as she stood with her case at her feet. She looked inland. The sun was from that direction, so a halo sat over the greenery. She shaded her eyes, seeing no mountains, no volcanoes, just thick jungle. But then she made out the pinky-coloured walls of a villa. Wow, she thought, quite impressed. She shouldered her bag and picked up her case, looking again. In front of the villa stood a line of palm trees, each one stereotypically on a slant, and beyond that there was a collection of thatched beach huts where she assumed there would be a bar for group visitors. Then, from between these huts, came striding a dark figure. Janet! Finally. Here was the staff/concierge/security, whatever.

Nancy walked off the rocky area and over the adorable white sand, heading for a rendezvous with Janet. How surreal, she thought, grinning. She longed for that drink.

Janet, still at distance, was dark skinned, although Nancy didn't think she was a West Indian lady. She looked quite butch, actually. She was wearing a black shirt and black shorts. As she got closer, Janet's facial features began to form, causing Nancy to stop dead in her tracks. Janet was a man! *What the fuck*!?

Fight or flight adrenalin flooded through Nancy's body, but, seeing as she had nowhere to run to, it was the former that occupied her mind. The man was waving. He was smaller than her, acting in quite a friendly manner. Still, she felt stupid for putting herself in that situation. *Nancy!* Then the man stopped and stared.

'Nancy?' he called, sounding genuinely astonished. 'Is that you, Nancy?'

Nancy shielded her eyes again. It couldn't be? Could it? 'Eddi? Eddi!? What the absolute fuck are you doing here? Do you work here?'

Nancy was totally aghast, dropping her bag and closing the distance at a stumble through the sand. Eddi was smiling, equally puzzled. The strange man on the beach in a secluded Caribbean island was one man she knew she could give a hug to.

After the strong embrace, he stood back to stare at her.

'You work here!?' she asked again. 'Here, of all places?'

'No, I don't work here. I'm a guest. Wow.'

'A guest? I'm supposed to have it all to myself. Not that I'm complaining. Jesus, Eddi. Oh my God! Is it just you?'

'No, there are six of us. Nancy, there must have been some kind of booking mayhem.'

Nancy could not take her eyes of him. Off Eddi, her one-time boyfriend from Indonesia. Little, adorable, cute Eddi. Her brain finally began to accept the surprise. Okay, so be it. Bizarre, but it was a small world.

Eddi took her suitcase and they began walking off the beach.

'I saw the chopper,' he explained. 'Decided to come out and meet it. Nancy Niven, as I live and breathe.'

'My God, Eddi. Are you still a chef?'

Eddi paused as he considered his kitchen porter job in London.

'Yeah, yeah, working at a big hotel in East London.'

'You're back in London? Oh, Eddi. I was so nasty to you. I'm so sorry.'

'Hey, it's okay. We were very young, back then.'

They walked between the palm trees and between two of the quite large thatched buildings, in which she did, indeed, see a bar, and a Jacuzzi. A Jacuzzi overlooking the sea.

'Up these steps,' said Eddi, guiding her. 'I think everyone is in the villa.'

'Have you been here long?'

'No, just a couple of days.'

Nancy looked back at such a beautiful view. An image of Daniel back in New York flashed to her, as he ripped someone to shreds over the booking fiasco. But she was open-minded as to what she would find in the villa.

'I really need a drink, Eddi.'

Eddi, as a Muslim, didn't drink alcohol. Now, he knew some English Muslims who drank, but during those astonishing nine or ten months back in 2008 with Nancy it had been a shock to find that she liked her alcohol. It was the only thing that could have possibly put him off her. That and her teenage mood swings, of course.

'There's plenty to drink,' he assured her.

As the modern, pink villa loomed above her, there was only the sound of birdsong all around. They stepped into the cool portico. Eddi suggested they leave the bags there for a moment.

'Come on in, I'll introduce you.'

'Lead on. I can't wait.'

It was gloomy, but ornate. Marble floors, pot plants. Ahead, it was brightly lit, a massive lounge area, and beyond that a bespoke, stainless steel kitchen. She could see one or two heads bobbing about on sofas. As Eddi led her in, she saw a wide staircase, with a pair of flip-flops coming down, attached to hairy male legs and shorts, and someone jumped to their knees on a sofa, and someone else stood up. Another person came in from a decking area. Nancy let her eyes adjust. It took a few seconds.

'Everyone,' called Eddi. 'This is Nancy. She's just arrived. You'll never guess who she is.'

'Hello, Nancy,' said the man who was kneeling on the sofa.

Nancy's face felt like it had dropped to the floor. She was so staggered that she felt instantly nauseous. Like Eddi, the man was another Ex. The man was Ryan, a quite recent boyfriend from New York. Not the greatest relationship in the world. She could have done with never seeing him ever again in her life.

And there was Ex, Michael, on the stairs, another mistake from her time in the US. He crossed his tattooed, muscular forearms and grinned at her.

Ex, Francesco, was the one who had come in from outside, smiling his cheeky Italian smile. Fucking Francesco, her fling from a skiing season. Being an expressive Italian male, he could not hide his astonishment to see her there. He said something in Italian but her shock was blocking out all sound. He made some hand gestures which ended with his right hand sitting down the front of his shorts. Nancy managed a little, confused wave at him.

Now, Ex, Tommy stood up. Tommy from London, looking at her with almost aggression on his face; Jesus, what a nightmare to see Tommy there – to see Tommy at all.

Nancy didn't know what to do. Panic and confusion swamped her brain. Her knees felt weak. It was a waking nightmare. The party from hell. They were all there. All her romantic life was there from seventeen onwards. All except Jason Ikin. Beautiful, stupid Jason Ikin.

'Hello, Nancy.'

Out of the kitchen came the cherry on the cake. Kelly, her Ex-girlfriend from university, bold as brass in a tiny white bikini, looking hot, cocktail in hand. Nancy had forgotten about Kelly a long time ago.

If Eddi had not taken her into an embrace, Nancy would have sunk to her knees or run out to the beach.

15

Slightly reluctantly due to his religion, Eddi provided the beer which Nancy drank, as she sat on a lounger in one of the thatched huts near to the beach. The shock was dissipating, though her mind continued to work feverishly. Eddi was there with her, holding her hand. He had already tried to dab away her tears with a tissue, for which she had thanked him and kissed his cheek.

'What's happening here, Eddi? Why am I brought together with people from my past?'

'I don't know, sweetheart. I really don't know. Please don't cry. I don't like to see you cry.'

Nancy let out a frustrated little scream. Then she tried to calm her breathing.

'How... how did you come to be here?' she asked.

'Well, let me think, I received a cheque for £10,000 and a plane ticket. Not something I was going to turn down. I think all the others had similar things happen to them. None of us knew of any connection to you.'

'What did you think when you got the money?'

'I thought it was a joke, at first. There was some firm's name on the cheque, I didn't recognise. But the cheque cleared. I flew out. I thought it was some kind of secret benefactor. You know, like that TV programme, *Secret Millionaire*, or the one where the boss goes undercover in his firm, then does nice things for his staff. Nancy, I would have contacted you immediately if I knew anything of this.'

She squeezed his hand. 'I know you would have, darling.'

She drank her beer. Another image of Daniel came to her, this time bringing his lawyers into things. Fuck, never mind lawyers, she wanted the police.

'I want to radio the people in charge of the island.'

'Nothing's happening on the radio, Nancy. We've tried that already.'

'You mean... I'm stuck here?'

Someone approached. Francesco. He gave her a plate of sandwiches, and sat himself down, uninvited. Nancy was ravenous, so started to eat.

'Well, well,' he said, pulling his hair back. 'Very strange, Nancy, girl.'

'Hello, Francesco. Yes, very strange.'

'It's lovely to see you.'

'How's your Mamma?'

'She's very well.'

'She's not here, is she?'

'Unfortunately not. But I'm here. I look after you.'

'I'm fine, thank you.'

'People in there want a meeting with you.' He shrugged.

'Personally, I'm not bothered. They want to talk it through, they say.'

'I'm very happy here, thank you very much.'

'You can't stay here all night.'

Eddi agreed with Francesco. 'He's right, Nancy. Please come inside.'

Francesco said, 'That girl, Kelly, has prepared you a room.'

So, Nancy was persuaded back into the villa. There was no music, no television. There was nobody in the lounge or kitchen. She wandered outside with Eddi and Francesco, looking down across a cultured lawn to a swimming pool, where Tommy and Michael frolicked with Kelly. Clearly, they were not going to let bizarre reality disturb their free vacation. To the left, on the patio, stood an outdoor pool table where Ryan was hitting balls. He stood up and stared at her.

'Why are you here, Ryan?' she asked, with a touch of hostility in her voice.

'I'm an actor, Nancy. I'm supposed to be here shooting a commercial. I don't know what the fuck is going on.'

That made Nancy think of something; perhaps she had been thrown into some kind of reality television show. Maybe there were hidden cameras everywhere. Did they think she could be played like that? Someone, somewhere, was going to jail. No, going to jail after giving her $20m and a grovelling apology.

The holiday scene was too much for her. Her head was banging. No meeting seemed about to be convened. She turned to Eddi.

'Yes, babe?' he asked.

'I want to go to this room that's been prepared for me. I want you to stay with me, Eddi.'

Nancy woke, still in her clothes, on the King size bed. She knew she had been dreaming, but waking up with a start had dispelled the dream instantly. She sat up and rubbed her eyes. Lace curtains rippled at the windows, as if she were on the set of *The Great Gatsby,* or something.

No, the trip hadn't been part of the dream; Eddi sat slumped in a chair, fast asleep. She really was there with six Exes. But now she was refreshed, and there was more anger flowing through her, instead of shock. She thought things through. Clearly, all six of them were as puzzled as she was. She decided not to antagonise them, but to build up some kind of relationship again, just to be able to find a way to contact the authorities. Maybe they weren't alone on the island. She and Eddi could walk to another villa for help.

She got up gingerly and walked out through the blowing curtains onto the balcony. It was an overcast morning. Only two of her fellow vacationers were visible; Tommy and Francesco, doing exercises in shorts and little vests. Even from fifty feet away she could see their back muscles being used, and Tommy's butt cheeks were clenched tight against his shorts. Francesco's attire represented Inter Milan football team, which briefly threw her back to that ski season in Madesimo, until she shook her head and left them to it.

Nancy inspected the en suite facilities, finding them spotlessly clean. The row of toiletries were quality products. After showering, she put the same clothes back on, as she had no intention of giving the impression that she was staying. She looked at her bodyguard, so sweet in his sleep, then went downstairs to find some food. After that, Eddi would be woken and they would walk out to try to find another occupied villa.

Downstairs, there was nobody immediately to face up to. It allowed her to assess the living quarters of the villa properly, not in her professional capacity, just to see the sofas arranged around a wood burning stove, and the way the kitchen flowed into the outside area. On one side of the lounge was a picture window showing a full panorama of the sea. She allowed herself to enjoy that for a moment. *Wow.* Then she wandered about some more, seeing corridors leading off to what she assumed were bedrooms and bathrooms. Empty beer bottles and dirty food plates were littered about everywhere, which summed up a few of her Exes. *Pigs.* There were unwashed pots in the kitchen sink. She found a croissant and looked in the fridge, which was fully stocked with bottles of beer, fruit juice, soft drinks, and bottles of champagne. She took some cheese.

Approaching flip-flops alerted her to her first confrontation of the new day. Kelly came to a floppy stop on seeing her there. She was in a little white tee-shirt, into which her great breasts strained, with a sarong, and sunglasses on top of her head. It was awkward for a second, then she came on for a little hug.

'It's nice to see you, Nancy. Whatever the circumstances.'

Nancy backed off a little way, nibbling her croissant. 'Kelly.'

'Did you sleep well? You've been away from us for twelve hours.'

'I slept fine, thank you.'

Kelly continued to the fridge for a can of Coke. A strawberry caught her attention and she started eating that. Nancy looked at Kelly's hair and her skin. It must be nearly nine years since she had seen Kelly, and she looked the same age as before. If any of what was happening could be founded in logic, then Kelly, secret lesbian lover from university, was a mystery participant. How was she not lost in the fog of time?

Nancy did not feel like playing the Private Investigator again, remembering her plan to build up some kind of working relationship with these people in order to facilitate a resolution. So, instead, she decided to speak politely to Kelly.

'What have you been up to since Uni?'

'Oh, various things. Worked in advertising. Modelling. Got married. Got divorced. Now I'm... back modelling. Television work.'

'Television?'

'Oh, only one of those hardly watched satellite channels. Anyway, you?'

'I work in Real Estate. In New York.'

'No way? New York? That's great. Hey, come outside.' Nancy followed behind. 'There's only those two dickheads working-out on the lawn. I don't know where Michael or the Indonesian bloke are?'

'Eddi's asleep in my room.'

Kelly laughed, looking over her shoulder, before dropping her sunglasses down. 'You're still a fast worker, I see.'

'He slept in a chair.'

'Whatever.'

They took seats on the patio. To her left, beyond the corner of the villa, Nancy could see a strip of ocean and a curve of the beach, and to her right stood thick jungle. But also to the right, stood a self-contained building, with a thatched roof like the huts on the beach. Nancy knew it was overflow accommodation but her imagination turned it into some sort of love nest.

The floorshow currently had Tommy and Francesco doing sit-ups. Nancy looked at Kelly again, at the curves of her breasts, remembering, remembering.

'So, do we have to discuss conspiracy theories?' asked Kelly.

'No, we don't have to talk about anything.'

'Good. It's a lovely place here.'

'I *was* quite looking forward to it.'

'Do you think you can relax and enjoy it?'

Nancy guffawed. 'Sorry. So, you're happy here? Where are you living in England?'

'Still in London. I don't think I'll ever leave London. I have a nice apartment. I drive a Porsche. Four years old but still...'

'Remember when we both decided to get Porsches? Because that posh boy, Nigel, had one. Do you keep in touch with anyone from those times?'

'Well, I married Nigel.'

'You didn't!?'

'No!'

They both laughed. It caused Tommy and Francesco to take notice and come posing in front of them. Francesco tossed his heavy dark curls.

'I suppose it could be worse,' joked Kelly, indicating the guys. 'Look at their tats, Nancy.'

Nancy huffed, thinking about Leo. 'A bit amateurish.'

'You cheeky mare,' said Tommy. 'What do you mean amateurish?' He flexed his biceps, indicating Roman Numerals, then there was script on his left rib cage, which he kindly lifted his top to show. 'Woman, I remember you liked tracing your fingertips around my tattoos.'

Nancy moodily looked off into the trees. 'Don't remind me.'

Francesco whipped off his top to show his own Roman Numerals across his chest, then turned to show the image on his back.

'Who is that of?' asked Kelly. 'Your mother?'

'Hey!' objected Francesco, grinning. 'Bitch. Never be rude about Mamma. This image is of Zlatan Ibrahimovic. Admittedly, he was not with us very long, but what a great footballer.'

'Hey, Frankie!' called Michael, emerging from the forest, right through the legs of the Love Nest, with Ryan trailing behind.

Francesco did a double-take. 'Is he talking to me?'

Nancy looked, seeing the two big-balled, American fucks in their typical, back-to-front baseball caps.

'Put your man boobs away, Frankie,' Michael continued. 'We've found something!'

16

Nancy reluctantly allowed Kelly to pull her to her feet, protesting that she thought it best if she were allowed to go get Eddi.

'No, let the man sleep,' said Kelly. 'Come on.'

The men were already trekking away into the jungle. Kelly actually kept hold of Nancy's hand as they skipped after them, something which stirred dormant emotions deep within Nancy, so she shook herself free by the time they ducked through the branches.

They headed uphill. Birds twittered and the sun flickered through the foliage. It was fairly humid. The boys started bantering, Tommy saying it had better be worth it, with lots of swear words being exchanged. The girls fell behind a little way, but when they heard excited yells, they rushed on into a clearing, to find a large wooden building. It reminded Nancy of a ski hut, out of which the slalom skiers would depart. The boys were clambering over side walls or running around to the entrance. Nancy and Kelly looked in through a window, seeing just a concrete floor.

'I'm none the wiser,' said Kelly.

They moved around to the front, and it all became clear; a ribbon of concrete curved away from an open, covered area, before it disappeared down into the tree line. Just inside the front of the building sat a number of go-carts, with the four boys excitedly examining them and trying to find how they started up.

'These are fucking excellent!' exclaimed Tommy. 'Fucking excellent!'

Kelly tutted. 'Your other English Ex is just so uncouth. Whatever did you see in him?'

Tommy laughed and answered for her, 'This!' He grabbed his groin and gave it a crude, upwards pull.

Nancy ignored him, stepping into the pavilion, where Francesco was sitting down into one of the go-carts.

'Darling, Nancy, hey, are you up for a ride?' he asked her, smiling.

Nancy crossed her arms. 'No, I'm not.'

Michael announced to everyone that he was into bikes, that he understood the go-carts and, sure enough, he soon had them all roaring into life. Francesco volunteered to go down first.

'What's this, a brave fucking Italian!?' laughed Tommy, his right hand now resting down inside the front of his shorts.

Francesco gave the Englishman the finger, before setting off, via four squeaky bumps on the kerbs.

'I wouldn't want him behind me,' joked Ryan.

'That's how he used to fuck Nancy,' said Tommy, causing him and Ryan to laugh madly.

'Who's next?' asked Michael.

Kelly raised her hand, jumping forward with girly excitement, before squatting down into one of the little vehicles. Michael admired her legs as they stuck out from the sarong, then gave her a quick lesson on the pedals. Then she was off in a puff of petrol smoke, giving a little wave to Nancy.

Tommy insisted on going next, pushing his bright yellow machine into position. He was chanting something above the growl of the little 2 stroke engine as he took the first bend on the concrete track, before dropping away into the trees.

'Only two carts left,' pointed out Michael.

'I'll walk back,' said Nancy.

She was amazed and disgusted with herself for how disappointed she felt to be missing out on the fun.

'No, you won't,' said Ryan, already sitting himself down. 'Get on with me.'

She stared at him. She imagined sitting on his lap, his strong arms holding her in, as he guided them down the course. She would be lying back into his chest, feeling his hot breath on her neck, bumping around on his crotch and surely making him big.

'No, you're all right,' she said, turning on her heels and heading back the way she had come.

Ryan shrugged, connected fists with Michael and off he went.

Michael watched Nancy thoughtfully until she was swallowed up by the trees. He took the last machine, which was red and with number seven on the face plate, and followed everyone down. Once out of the clearing, the track began to twist and turn, becoming quite risky at points, thoroughly good fun. There was a pointless wooden tunnel and a bridge over a stream, before a tight bend, where he passed a kneeling Francesco with his overturned cart, after a crash, then bursting into the sunshine, promenading along the beach for a few seconds before the climb back up to the hut. Brilliant! Absolutely brilliant! He would have to get something similar, back home in the States.

'Aku tadi khawatir sama kamu, waktu aku nangun kamu tidak ada!', called Eddi from the kitchen, as he saw Nancy emerge from the trees. He was drinking coffee and excavating sleep from his eyes. Nancy's Indonesian was shamefully limited, but she knew he was saying something about being frightened for her well-being, when he woke to find her gone.

'Sorry, my husband.'

She jogged up to join him.

'Have you been looking for other villas?' he asked.

'No, the other... err... my Exes have found a go-cart track up in the hills. I was just watching them.'

That news excited him. 'A go-cart track? Really?'

'Go and have a drive, if you want.'

'No, no, you want to go looking for other people. I've packed some supplies for our expedition.'

'Oh? You're so good. Shall we go now?'

Eddi nodded, keen to do that. They both put on small backpacks, and went out through the front of the villa.

'Listen,' said Eddi, 'any other villas will be beachfront, I assume.

So I suggest we keep walking the shore and see what we come to.'

'That's a brilliant idea. Thank God you're here, Eddi.'

Eddi gave her a slightly embarrassed smile.

Nancy walked alongside Eddi, there on a beach in the Caribbean, and it was totally surreal. She assumed she was in some kind of temporary denial over the situation, because she had switched her mind off from it. But it was just so nice out there, with not a cloud in the sky, clean white sand moving over her trainers with every step. She had once been with Eddi to a few beaches in Indonesia, when they were so, so young. The memory made her grin and she sneaked a look at his fresh face. Had Kuta Beach and Peucang Island been nicer than this location? Ahh, she just savoured a breeze which moved her wild hair about her face. He looked. She listened to the sound of the surf. She was happy, despite the insanity of what was happening. Maybe, if they found other people on the island, her anger would flood back and she would forget the beautiful surroundings and demand to be rescued.

Eddi helped her over the rocks at the far right curve of the bay before they moved on. The trees thinned and quite a wide stretch of the island lay there before them, with one white building glinting in the distance.

'Let's head there first,' said Nancy, before she suddenly stopped walking.

'What's wrong?' he asked.

'A bit embarrassing, but I think I should have gone for a pee before we left. I'll just...'

While Nancy scooted off into some long grass, Eddi gentlemanly turned his gaze out to sea.

On the walk back from the go-carts (which were such fun they might just have to be used every day), it was Kelly who raised the topic they had all been ignoring.

'So, guys, any clues about our girl, Nancy?'

The four men stopped joking about and reliving their driving experiences, and Francesco stopped looking at his grazed hands and forearms from his accident. None of them had anything constructive to say to Kelly.

'Super,' she said, with heavy sarcasm. 'Well, I estimate, in my supermarket shopping capacity, that we have about two weeks of supplies. After that we better get picked up or start swimming. I don't want to spend my birthday here.'

'Oh, it's your birthday soon?' asked Tommy. 'Is there anything you want for a present?' He and Francesco giggled. 'My last girlfriend,' continued Tommy, 'asked for something different for her birthday. I looked into getting some sexy panties made special, with my name stitched backwards on the waistband. So, after a long day in the office, she can strip them off and see my name branded into her hips.' He laughed uproariously.

'You pig,' said Kelly.

17

Tommy dived head first into the swimming pool. On surfacing, he docked at the side and wiped water from his eyes. He took his time looking at a sunbathing Kelly, estimating that her bikini contained about twenty per cent less fabric than any woman he had ever been abroad with. The bottoms were debatably indecent, not quite showing flesh at the sides of her sex but hinting that she kept herself shaved. It crossed his mind to ask that very question; he normally would have done, but after several days out there in the Caribbean he still felt low in confidence, unsure with how things had panned out.

At first, he had ignored the solicitor's letters. Then his mother, who lived nearby and was always in and out of his flat, insisting on doing his ironing, made him follow it up. So he met with Younger, Kennedy or Martinson (he didn't pay much attention to which one), at their offices in Watford town centre, and was informed of what was on offer. Nothing else was forthcoming; no reasons, no strings attached. It all seemed very strange. Massively strange, in fact. He couldn't figure it out at all. He went out with his mates, but could not find a way to drop the subject into the conversation. Then he got pissed and necked on with a fit dental assistant he met in a club. Three days later, he had his money and his ticket. What the hell.

Kelly was running it through her head again at the same time as Tommy. A Private Investigator had found her, one night, at work in the warehouse studio. Once he had got past security and even got around her artistic name of Kendall, he had delivered his message. At first she had thought she was in serious trouble. But then she heard the man out. The offer was extremely tempting. It crossed her mind that a rich Arab had seen her performing on the show, that she was being kidnapped to be in his harem. A few days later she knew a lot more about it, and she was not the kind of woman to look a gift horse in the mouth.

Michael and Ryan were nearby, making fishing rods from bamboo garden poles. It was not a panicked response to Kelly's assessment of their supply situation, but that had been the reason for their thinking up the trip to the surf the following morning. Both men had received similar visits from Private Investigators, Michael at his condominium in Miami just before he was to leave on a modelling assignment and Ryan while working on a television commercial in LA.

'Kelly, you know when you were talking about supplies?' asked Tommy. 'That was food, right? Not alcohol?'

'That's right, Tommy. Months and months of alcohol.'

She put down her glass of wine and picked up her cell phone, which was stuffed inside a toy onesie in the form of a panda bear.

There was absolutely no signal for anything on the phone but she just felt she needed to hold it.

'I've never seen anything like that before,' said Tommy.

'My little onesie?' giggled Kelly. 'It's fun, isn't it? My friend bought it for me. She's got a zebra one.'

Tommy laughed.

'Kelly, what's for *tea*?' asked Michael.

'If you think I'm cooking every night, Yankee boy, you've got another think coming. But there are steaks in the fridge. Maybe you could sort out the barbie?'

Michael nodded. If something needed doing, he could do it.

'I thought the Indonesian fella was a chef?' asked Kelly.

'His name's Eddi,' said Tommy.

'Whatever. I can't even remember your name, sonny boy. Right, I'll do my back now.' For a woman used to going semi-nude, and simulating sex in front of several hundred thousand viewers, she was remarkably coy in the way she turned over and then undid her bikini string.

The three men there watched the manoeuvre with fascination, before returning to their hobby craft and swimming, respectively.

Francesco, his forearms bandaged with several little plasters after his go-cart accident, was inside, taking extraordinary care over the Espresso machine. When his Italian sensibilities were satisfied that his drink was perfect, he sat down on one of the sofas. It was very quiet in the villa. He tossed his curly locks and looked about him, wishing there was a TV. Even US television would suit his need to be entertained. Normally, he liked adventure holidays which included wind surfing or mountain biking. But he was happy there, not having to work, enjoying the weather and free bed and board. Official letters had started arriving for him at Mamma's hotel in Madesimo, which he received and read, so when the Private Eye from Turin turned up, he was ready to listen. He could never have guessed it all involved some strange little experiment with that fun, little chalet maid from one ski season, long forgotten.

In through the front entrance came Nancy and Eddi, both trailing their empty rucksacks behind them on the floor.

'Ciao!' called Francesco, smiling broadly, glad of the company.

'Right back at you,' said Nancy, in a lifeless tone, heading straight to the fridge. 'I've never walked so bloody far in my entire life.'

She took two bottles of water, giving one to Eddi, and they crashed out, facing Francesco.

'Any luck?' asked Francesco, leaning forward with hands on his knees.

Nancy slaked her thirst. God, she needed to get out of those clothes. She felt filthy. 'Not really,' she answered.

'You mean we're all alone?'

'We found two other properties. Both unoccupied, and with no provisions. No radios, that we could find, anyway.'

'Any boats?'

She crinkled her delicate brows at him. 'You want to go out to sea?'

'No, I suppose not.'

Michael came in. He was in shorts, an *Abercrombie & Fitch* tee-shirt and black mules. Nancy glanced, unable to deny he looked hot. He blatantly eyed up the dishevelled Nancy in her sprawled out position, then checked on the steaks in the fridge. 'I'm doing steaks for *tea*,' he said, again emphasising the English term for dinner. 'Is that okay?' Francesco nodded, Eddi managed to raise a tired arm into a thumbs up. 'Nancy?'

'I suppose I've got to eat.'

He took a beer, opened it without caring where the top flew, and went back outside.

'So, which one of us was there first?' asked Tommy, now sitting in the sun by the pool.

'What's that?' asked Michael, returning.

'Which one of us had Nancy first?'

Kelly replied without looking up, 'I knew her at university. Both eighteen years old.'

'We will be hearing all about that?' Tommy asked, grinning at the other two boys.

'Sure. We'll get around to it, no doubt.'

'Well,' said Michael, 'Me and Ryan knew her in the last couple of years, in the States.'

Tommy was thinking. 'I'm a bit later than Kelly. Shame it wasn't at the same time.'

'In your dreams,' said Kelly.

Tommy continued, 'Maybe Eddi was first, being the same nationality. I don't know about Francesco.'

Kelly sat up and turned. 'I wonder who she found the best?'

They all laughed. Laughter which died away as Nancy, Eddi and Francesco came out to sit on the patio.

'Nancy and Eddi have walked around the island,' announced Francesco. 'There's no-one else here.'

They all gave that some consideration.

'So,' said Nancy, 'I'm stuck with you... people.'

'Might as well get in the pool, then,' joked Tommy.

18

Nancy sat up in bed, stretching out and yawning in a very unladylike fashion. She sniffled a little bit. Due to her allergies, she was an unsettled sleeper, once waking an Ex up in the middle of the night with the noise she was making, prompting him to call her a snorter. She sniffled again. But she actually felt all right, and she found the smell of the ocean to be quite intoxicating. She was wearing a flimsy pink top and a pair of white panties, and wondered if not bringing her pyjamas was now to be considered a mistake on her part. The only sound she could hear were the birds in the trees. She looked down at the lean, yet toned back of Eddi, as he slept on, beside her. His face was turned towards the ceiling and she assessed that his stubble was more masculine than when she had first known him. There was a little scar on his chin, possibly from his work in the professional kitchen. He was more of a man now, handsome and cute, if not totally in the Alpha male category of the others in the villa.

Tearing her eyes away from his lovely skin, she headed to the bathroom to shower. When she came out later, rubbing her hair dry, Eddi was still well away, so she dressed and left him alone. Downstairs, she could see Ryan, Michael and Francesco doing sit-ups out on the lawn. *Good grief.*

'Morning,' called Kelly, working away at the stove. She was wearing a bikini, encased at the front by a stripy apron.

'Good morning.'

'There's coffee in the pot. I'm making Egg in Bread. Want some? You remember my Egg in Bread from Uni days?'

'I'll have some, please.'

'Sit yourself down. I've just had a brainstorming session with those three about why we're here. It was a very short meeting, and we decided not to discuss it again.'

'Sounds like a good plan.'

'I've not seen the Indonesian bloke.'

'Eddi. He's asleep in my bed.'

'Oh, really?'

Once again, Nancy saw no reason to explain how Eddi had stayed with her platonically in her bed. That they had briefly cuddled, and that he had been a perfect gentleman. Kelly's French toast, or Egg in Bread, as she preferred to call it, arrived in front of Nancy and she devoured it ravenously. Kelly sat down with her own plate. Both girls eyed each other over their forks.

'So, what now?' asked Kelly.

'What now? Well, I'm over the shock. I've just decided this is some weird, sick joke, and I'm going to ignore everyone and have my vacation until someone official shows up.'

'Now, *that* sounds like a plan.'

The three boys all came in from the garden, each carrying a fishing pole. In turn they looked at Nancy, before they collected snacks and drinks from the fridge and headed out the front way.

'They're going fishing,' explained Kelly.

'Keeps them out of trouble, I suppose. Thank you for breakfast. It was nicer in your digs, as I remember.'

Kelly shrugged.

Nancy decided on a thorough tour of the villa and its grounds. First she wandered over the lawns, seeing the tennis courts. Then she ascended into the solidly-built Love Nest, which felt like a tree house for grown-ups. There was a seating area overlooking the ocean, an outdoor barbecue, and several camp beds, plus a hammock. She liked it greatly. Back inside the main villa, there were marble floors throughout. Every area had an ornate wooden fan hanging from the ceiling, although there was air-conditioning. She found two downstairs bedrooms along a corridor from the lounge, each with en-suite bathrooms. Judging by the clothes spread around, it was the two Americans in those rooms. In the second room she picked up a discarded bath robe which bore the initials MK. Michael's. She sniffed it before letting it drop.

There was a bathroom off the foyer, and a matching one right above it as she ascended the stairs. Her bedroom was first, then three others. She poked her head into each one, easily recognising Kelly's by her female belongings, while not being sure which ones belonged to Francesco and Eddi. While upstairs at the front, she viewed the stunning panoramic view of the ocean. Not a rescue boat in sight. The strip of white sand, occasionally blocked by palm leaves, showed the three fishermen heading off towards the rocks. Nancy briefly imagined them being swept to a watery grave.

Back letting her eyes enjoy panning across the sea, she thought of loved ones, and of New York, and of Leo Rooney. She was okay, she told herself. She had Eddi. Everyone else was a waking nightmare, but they were at least being civil to her. It was time to get on with her vacation, if for no other reason than to help pass the time. She sneaked into her room, seeing Eddi still asleep. She picked her navy blue bikini and quickly slipped into it with her back to the bed. She pulled her flip flops from her case, threw a tee-shirt on, and headed down for her first use of the pool.

'So, what's New York like?' asked Kelly, sitting by the swimming pool.

Nancy expressed her opinion on the greatest city on earth, then resumed her breaststrokes, up and down the pool.

'I think I'd like to visit,' said Kelly. 'If only I could afford it. I don't think I could live there. London's mad enough for me. So, are you dating?'

Nancy just gave a simple negative shake of the head in passing. 'You?' she asked, coming back.

'Not at the moment.' After a pause, she laughed. 'I just imagined telling my last fella that I was going to the Caribbean. He was a bit of a miser. We would have ended up fighting. Are you on good money in New York? I bet you are.'

'I can't complain. You must be earning as a model?'

'I'm doing all right, I suppose. There's something else I want to ask you?'

'Why be shy now?'

'This Indonesian bloke?'

'Eddi! His name's Eddi.'

'Eddi, yes, I must remember. Did you know him before me?'

Nancy stopped swimming. 'Why?'

'Just wondered. I don't remember you ever mentioning him.'

'I'm pretty sure I did. I met Eddi during a family trip to Jakarta. When I was seventeen. He was a school friend of a cousin of mine.'

Nancy hauled herself out of the pool. Kelly looked at the slim beauty, dripping onto the grass, squeezing her black mane of hair over her right shoulder. Her skin was a light tan colour, even lighter where her smaller bikini bottoms revealed where her panties had been. Nancy looked straight at Kelly. God, thought Kelly, she remembered that body. She remembered those flitting black eyes.

'What?' asked Nancy. 'Did you think you were my first lover?'

19

Nancy had chosen Kingston University, London because it meant she could still live at home, there being no great urge for freedom, unlike with most teenagers. Kelly Higginbottom picked it because they were running her Drama, Dance, Film, TV, Media and Music course, and moving out of her dysfunctional family home in Aldershot, with her always angry, always drunk, soldier stepfather, was a bonus.

The two girls met one humid summer evening at a party in a flat overlooking the Thames river. They had seen each other around the campus, so conversation came easily after being introduced by mutual friends. At first, they talked Uni stuff, fashion, and about the boys spread out through the flat. Nancy had actually necked on recently with Alistair Franklin, the captain of the lacrosse team and quite an up and coming name in Triathlon, so very fit, and Kelly had been impressed. The two girls had giggled about it.

Those mutual friends soon forgot them, as their own boyfriends arrived, but Nancy and Kelly were very happy to keep chatting. Due to the evening's balmy temperature, and the party music being very loud, they picked up more Bacardi Breezers from the ice bin in the kitchen and found a spot out on a balcony.

As always, Nancy had to explain her Indonesian/English roots. That was so cool in Kelly's opinion, saying how she could only dream of having Nancy's exotic skin tone, which caused Nancy to blush. Kelly asked if it was okay for Nancy to drink, and was put right on the religious point. Their jean-clad lower legs were overlapping, such an inconsequential thing, but Nancy found herself thrilled by it, fascinated with Kelly. Kelly carried more confidence about her than Nancy; she knew what she was about. In Kelly's opinion, this Nancy was so cute. That uncontrollable, raven hair. She wanted to kiss that pure skin. She wanted to take her back to her student flat around the corner and take her to bed. But she had to be patient and play it right.

They agreed to meet for coffee, later in the week. More intimate chatting ensued. Great company. They were friends now, definitely. They went out clothes shopping. They went to the bar most frequented by the students. They caught the latest Tom Hardy film. Nancy was invited over to the flat where Kelly, having kicked her flatmates out for the night, cooked a beef joint, with roast potatoes and four types of veg. Their first embrace came as a result of Nancy's delight that Kelly had actually cooked for her. The hug in the kitchen lingered on, feeling so good, until they broke apart for air.

Kelly had always known she was bi-sexual, throughout school, bringing girlfriends, as well as boyfriends home, providing plenty of opportunities for leering and unpleasant jokes from the stepfather.

At Uni, she had been with one girl, an actress on her course, but that had fizzled out fairly quickly. She was all ready with her seduction plans for adorable Nancy. After wine on the sofa, their first kiss had come. Passion flared, hands moving into their hair and tongues into mouths. After what she considered a sensitive amount of time, Kelly cupped Nancy's left breast. This caused Nancy to pause, watching the hand move up to caress her excited nipple, then take in the whole with a soft grope. She continued kissing, but she wasn't ready for anything more, and Kelly sensed it. At first, being the girl from the rough estate in Aldershot, Kelly pressed on, working on the buttons to Nancy's blouse. But the stage was reached where Nancy had frozen, so Kelly stopped, chastised herself silently, then assured Nancy that there was no rush. Nancy felt so relieved. They continued kissing. There was more cuddling. They laughed at a drunken singer moving along the street outside. There was more kissing. It was all good, the ice broken. Nancy was in a taxi within half an hour.

A week went by without a text or a call, and both girls wondered if that was that. Nancy went out with her friends after classes. At home she helped her mother, and enjoyed spending time with her little sister. She started her driving lessons that week, as well. But then she and Kelly met in the canteen one lunchtime. There was that secret sparkle between their eyes and, on Nancy's side at least, a slight wetness between her legs. Kelly said she and some friends were going to see a dance performance. Would Nancy like to come along? She agreed. Good, the times were agreed on. The rest of the day allowed Nancy to think of nothing else but being out with Kelly.

A group of boys and girls took mini-buses to a theatre in Maidenhead. Nancy dressed conservatively in a black dress with black leggings. She sat alongside Kelly on the journey and in the theatre, and enjoyed the whole evening, although the dancing was the sort she had seen on *The X Factor* a million times and she spent most of the time checking out Kelly's profile in the gloom. There was no touching, and that was agonising for her.

Finally they got back to Nancy's home, with her family away for the weekend. It was Kelly's first visit, so, glass of wine in hand, she asked to be given the tour. She announced that everything was so clean and white. The carpets looked like they were made from ten thousand West Highland Terriers. Nancy laughed. Kelly could be so dramatic at times. There were gnarly beams everywhere and furniture that looked like it hadn't needed an Allen key and a lot of swearing to put it together. Kelly was so jealous. In fact, she told Nancy that her whole house in Aldershot would fit into her kitchen.

In Nancy's plush bedroom she thanked Kelly for inviting her out. Kelly caressed Nancy's face and played with her wild Asian hair. Nancy was nervous and that always made her black eyes flit around. Kelly found it an endearing characteristic. They kissed.

With the beautiful carpet in mind, Kelly carefully placed down their wine glasses before guiding Nancy down onto her bed. There was no plethora of teddy bears everywhere but it did squeak annoyingly. Kelly got above Nancy, making sure to fill her world, then she was kissing all around her neck and cheeks. Nancy was making little noises immediately, pulling Kelly's body against hers. Nancy was not completely inexperienced. She had necked on with boys from school, let them touch her, and it was not long since her first love affair with the boy in Indonesia. But Kelly was so amazing, so gorgeous, clearly much more experienced in lovemaking. She was so nervous, so Kelly paused to ask if she was allowed to continue, and she replied that her panties had never been so wet. The following day she would cringe at the statement but at the time it seemed right.

They undressed slowly, allowing each other's breasts to be kissed and sucked. Kelly saw the wet panties and Nancy crawled into a ball of embarrassment, until she was kissed out of it. Kelly removed the offending panties and tossed them across the room. Kelly's fingers gently moved between Nancy's legs and had the expected effect. Kelly loved Nancy's pert breasts, unable to stop kissing them. She started to work her fingers, referring to Nancy's wet vulva as velvet. Shy Nancy begged to get into bed properly, so Kelly stood to make a big show of removing her own panties, at which point Nancy started to bite a finger at how sexy her friend looked. Kelly had a thin blonde line of pubes leading from her pussy. They jumped under the covers. Kissing and cuddling continued. When she could resist no longer, Kelly kissed her way down to Nancy's pussy.

20

'Why do you want me to stay in my bikini?' Nancy asked Kelly, later that day. 'We're only going to eat grilled fish, down on the beach.'

'Yes, Nancy, darling, but you are clearly unaware of the other pool down there. As it's still so hot, I thought you'd like to try it, that's all.'

'Oh. Okay. I'll just get something to go around me.'

'Put something of mine on. Come on, I've brought more stuff than you.'

After a little hesitation, Nancy followed Kelly up to her room. A selection of sarongs were held around Nancy's body by Kelly, her hands moving against Nancy's hips, with their faces only millimetres apart. Nancy picked one and allowed Kelly to attach it to her.

'There you are,' said Kelly. 'You look adorable.'

Nancy let the compliment go in one ear and out the other. 'Yeah, right, let's go.'

Michael and Ryan had gone ahead to get the barbecue started for the two fish which they had been amazed to catch that morning. Michael, who had been on a few fishing trips to the Caribbean before, assured them that the fish were edible and had prepared them himself, but there had been a couple of glances towards chef, Eddi, who had not volunteered his services. Perhaps he was one of those chefs who flat out refused to cook when he was on vacation, like a bus driver who refuses to drive.

Nancy walked down to the thatched beach huts with Eddi and Kelly. Francesco brought up the rear, carrying a large cool box containing alcohol.

'Champagne!' called Francesco, very animated. 'Who wants champagne?'

'Me!' replied Kelly, laughing over her shoulder at him.

Nancy checked on Eddi. 'Are you all right?'

'I'm good, Nancy. Thank you for asking.'

'I'm so hungry. I don't like this reality show much. I miss my favourite restaurants.'

They laughed, then ploughed on through the white sand. The sun was quite low in the sky, though still hot. Nancy could just about make out a cruise ship, or an oil tanker, on the horizon. Eddi led them to the left, along the beach edge, and there, between two huts and two leaning palm trees, was the most perfect infinity pool in the world. It beckoned Nancy. Nearby, smoke billowed up from the barbecue. Under any other circumstance it would have been ideal. Still, Nancy's tummy rumbled with hunger.

They sat about talking. Well, Nancy listened mostly. She was the only one, apart from Eddi, not drinking. Michael continued to check the fish, and the rice that he was steaming. Nancy watched him, liking his black vest and shorts, seeing his perfect smile as he grinned at something said by Ryan, followed by a high five. She checked out his muscle definition, watched the way he cooked, remembering the meals he had made her in his New York apartment; followed by the nights of rough lovemaking. He had been very vigorous, very in charge. She looked down at the twig she was moving about by her toes in the sand, thinking of Leo, of the time he pretended to be cooking for her, and of his wonderful, gentle but firm lovemaking afterwards. If only she had met the photographer as soon as she had moved to New York.

Soon, they were all served up a very appealing dish of food, which Nancy ate ravenously, as if she were a shipwreck survivor. There was much lip-smacking from the others and one or two compliments directed towards Michael. Nancy allowed Kelly to press a glass of champagne on her. It tasted exquisite with the food. The ocean at dusk was just something magical. Nancy sat back and listened to the conversations around her; the mannerisms of her Exes came back to her with every new minute she spent near to them. Tommy swore in every sentence – had that not bothered her when they dated? Ryan was clearly so incredibly vain, in just the way he sat, in the way he held his face, or constantly fussed with his hair. Yes, he had the best physique, the cutest looks, but didn't he just know it? Jeez, she thought, when did she become so knowing? So wise?

Francesco was trying to encourage Kelly to do without her sarong and get into the pool. Francesco was perhaps the most puzzling to Nancy. He was not what you would call a typical Italian male, despite the activity he was currently engaged in. He possessed hidden depths. There would never be any bottom pinching from Francesco, or riding by English soccer fans on a scooter to slash their buttocks with a razor. He could say silly things, play the fool, but deep down he was a sensible man. She watched Eddi offer his hand to guide Kelly into the pool. Adorable, straightforward, Eddi, and her devious Kelly. Do anything to get along in the world, Kelly. Kelly got into the pool with Francesco, with much flirting and laughter. Nancy looked over and watched Michael. The American was staring at the Italian, with no love lost there. Michael liked to be in control. It was his barbecue on the beach. His event. He felt he was the Alpha male. But then his expression softened. He turned on a few halogen lights around the pool, then took a beer and moved to sit next to Ryan. Yet *another* high five between the Americans made Nancy sit up and shake her head – it was like they were playing doubles tennis, or something. She wanted to get into that pool, so that's exactly what she did. The sarong came off. Everyone watched that, and despite herself, Nancy enjoyed the experience. Her adorable little butt was barely covered by the bottoms, and her small breasts moved as she took the three steps down. Eddi was offering a helping hand, then she reclaimed her champagne glass, which Tommy topped up. Although the light was going, she could feel that the pool appeared to go right out into the ocean. What a place. What a vacation.

'Kelly, what do you model?' asked Tommy.

Kelly grabbed both her breasts. 'I'm a hand model. I model hand cream and nail extensions. Haven't I got a fabulous pair of hands?'

'You have got a fucking fabulous pair of hands, babe,' agreed Tommy, laughing and downing his beer.

Francesco hopped out of the pool to get himself another drink. Everyone but Eddi was starting to get a little tipsy.

'Waiter,' said Tommy to Francesco. 'How are we for beer?'

Francesco took two fresh bottles out of the cool box and tossed one, quite firmly, to Tommy.

Nancy was having a little giggle to herself. Kelly noticed and pressed her to explain.

'Oh, I was just looking around at these huts. I used to be an estate agent in London. This one time I was selling a tiny terraced house for this African couple. Heavy wood furniture, tribal masks and spears on the walls. In the garden they had a complete thatched hut set up.'

'What was in it? A Jacuzzi?'

'No, nothing was in it. But it filled the small garden completely.'

'I bet the neighbours loved that.'

Their bizarre chat about the London property market was interrupted by Ryan and Michael stripping off their tops and slipping into the pool. Both girls watched, fascinated; Michael had more hair on his abdomen, but his six pack seemed slightly better defined. Ryan's chest and shoulders were larger. Nancy wondered if that came from football or boxing, maybe. His arms flexed like a gymnast on the rings as he lowered himself into the shallow end.

'What is it about tattooed men?' whispered Kelly.

Oh, don't, thought Nancy, instantly flashed back to being underneath the multi-coloured ink of Leo. Still, she checked her American Exes for their tattoos. Again, maybe it was that unusual situation in which she found herself, but she didn't remember assessing the boys too much when she was actually dating them. It was her busy life, no doubt, in the hustle and bustle of New York. When she got back she was definitely going to pay extraordinary attention to Leo Rooney.

Kelly touched her shoulder. 'How's your sister?'

'Lucy's good. She visited me recently in New York. You've got a sister, as I remember?'

'Mary, yeah. She's doing six months in Holloway for receiving stolen goods. Honestly. Anyway, it means I get to spend more time with my niece, who is being looked after around family members. Hey, she's had me doing one of those pat-a-cake games. Do you remember doing those growing up?' She laughed. 'Let me teach you.'

'No, you're all right.'

'Oh, come on, it will be fun. I think it's called Concentration, and you have to clap like this...'

Kelly proceeded to teach Nancy the routine, of double high fives followed by four rhythmic claps. 'This is... concentration... no repeats... or hesitation... the subject is...'

Nancy tried to get the timing right as they decided on a topic of words to be called out. They tried names of actresses, but collapsed into giggles as Brad Pitt got included. They tried animals, but Nancy lost the timing and their hands failed to connect. All the time the two American men watched in fascination.

'Carry On films,' said Kelly.

'I don't know any Carry On films,' protested Nancy.

'Of course you do.' The pat-a-cake started. 'This is Concentration... no repeats... or hesitation... the subject is... Carry On films. Camping.'

'Up The Khyber.'

'Cruising.'

'Doctor.'

'Follow That Camel.'

Nancy was struggling, both girls laughing. 'Cowboy!'

'Nurse.'

'Dick!'

The clapping failed in a burst of hilarity. Kelly took Nancy into a cuddle.

Away from the pool, Tommy and Francesco were talking.

'Yeah, but Italian football is slow compared to the English game,' Tommy was saying.

'But Italian football is more skilful,' answered Francesco.

'Bollocks. We've got the best players in the world. You haven't even got any fans at the games.'

'Not true.'

'Your game's riddled with corruption. What was it a couple of years ago? Inter Milan bribing officials.'

'No! That was Juventus.'

'Fucking Juventus. It was Inter. I remember. You got relegated two divisions over it.'

'It was Juventus!'

'Nah.'

'It was not my team doing the bribery!'

'Was.'

Francesco launched himself at Tommy's middle, taking him to the sand with a great oomph. As they manically grappled, they each tried to punch the other's head. Eddi was first there to try to separate them, quickly helped by Ryan and Michael leaping from the pool. Tommy continued to mouth off at the insulted Francesco as they were manhandled apart.

In the pool, Nancy looked on with a mixture of fascination and annoyance. She glanced at Kelly, who had a fingertip to her lips as she eagerly enjoyed every second of the testosterone wrestling match.

21

Nancy woke up all alone. The night before, Eddi had been so kind as to volunteer to join her again, but she was more her old self, by then, less shocked, independence rising. She was still puzzled, but no longer distressed at the bizarre situation.

She showered for a long time and washed her hair. While brushing her teeth, she realised that the white dressing gown she had put on after her shower bore her initials, like Michael's gown. At first, she absent-mindedly started to pick the stitching out, then left it alone. After a perfunctory towelling of her hair, she stepped out onto the balcony, finding the temperature to be pleasant enough. Noise took her attention to the tennis court, down below the lawn, where Tommy and Francesco were happily, if incompetently, playing a game their fight of the previous evening all forgotten. Below the balcony, Michael and Kelly were sunbathing. Nobody else was visible.

After doing her hair, Nancy put on a short, black cotton dress and flip flops and went downstairs. She found Eddi and Ryan in the process of washing every single pot and pan in the kitchen.

127

'Oh, what's this?' she enquired, getting herself a cup of coffee.

'Good morning, Nancy,' said a smiling Eddi. 'Kelly has made up a rota for cleaning. It's me and Ryan first.'

Nancy looked at Ryan, with his hands in the sink. He actually lifted a pink rubber-gloved hand to push hair out of his eyes with his wrist – in the six months she had been with him she had never once seen him wash up. Here was a typical, struggling actor, bumming around in all aspects of his life until he got that big break. Nancy remembered paying for most of their meals. The sex had been great, but there had been no true connection between them. Perhaps casting directors saw his lack of drive too. Still, Nancy found herself wanting to rest her head on Ryan's strong back, so finished making her coffee and flopped away.

She sat with her coffee in shade from the building, just as Francesco and Tommy came up from the court, all sweaty and elated Tommy having won some made-up form of the game. He had probably won 30 points to 20, thought Nancy, with two points for hitting a line.

'All right, bird?' said Tommy, on seeing Nancy.

Nancy made an aggressive cat sound at him, showing her teeth, which puzzled him for a moment. Both men sat near to Michael and Kelly. They already had bottles of water with them, which they used to slake their thirst. Nancy saw that Francesco had put his unruly hair up into a top knot.

'Good game?' asked Kelly, sitting up and putting her sunglasses on top of her head.

'I would have won,' complained Francesco, 'but for my bad knee, you understand, from a skiing accident when I was young.'

That was news to Nancy.

'Fuck that,' said Tommy. 'I've got my own old injuries. My left ankle is twice the size of the right.'

Michael sat up straight. 'I broke my ankle, too. Skydiving in Nevada.'

'Skydiving?' asked Tommy. 'Sod that for a game of soldiers. Kelly, have you got any old injuries to that perfect body of yours?'

Kelly readjusted her bikini bottoms in a very deliberate fashion. 'No, because I don't do silly sports.'

'Oh, look at this,' remembered Tommy, half turning to show a scar on the back of his left thigh, 'a burn from skipping a fire rope on the beach in Malaga.'

Nancy remembered the tale, explained to her in bed once. She rolled her eyes.

'Heaven preserve us,' despaired Kelly, inspecting the wound.

Tommy laughed. 'On the same holiday, one of my mates lost his front teeth doing a front somersault from a bollard. Landed in the sand, face first.' Tommy had a good laugh, then sighed. It was another day on this strange holiday. He looked at Eddi, who had just appeared outside. 'Are you cooking tonight, then, Eddi? Whip us up something special?'

All eyes turned to Eddi, who eventually nodded. 'Sure. Sure, no problem.'

In the afternoon, all the boys went on the go-carts again, and stayed there for several hours. Nancy went down to the beach. For the first time, following the trauma of her arrival, she felt she could really appreciate the natural beauty of the place. She walked on the beach and in the surf, picked up shells, allowed her hair to flow madly in the breeze. She gave a huge sigh as the warm wind took her breath away. If she ignored the nagging anxiety of her circumstances, she could lose herself in the total relaxation of her amazing vacation spot.

Wandering back, after more than an hour down there, she came across Kelly, bearing two glasses of fruit smoothies with straws. The infinity pool beckoned, so they put their drinks down on the edge and slipped in to the shallow end. Under the pretext that the boys were all far away and occupied, Kelly took off her bikini top. Nancy happened to be drinking at the time, so kept sucking, looking at Kelly's wonderful, perfectly-sized breasts. Superb, pointed, distracting breasts. Breasts that had come down to her mouth one Christmas Eve in a friend's spare room after a party, for example. She took off her own top. Her breasts were nice and small. Kelly didn't even look at them, just continued with her train of conversation. Nancy splashed her boobs. Still the woman wittered on while admiring the sea view.

'What?' asked Nancy. 'What did you just say?'

'I said I was starting to fancy Francesco. Would that be all right with you?'

'Fine. Knock yourself out. This place couldn't get any weirder for me.'

'He's walking about with his hair in that top knot today, and his beard is showing stronger.'

'Whatever.'

'So... are you having feelings for any of your exes again?'

Nancy looked at Kelly as if she were mad. Kelly bit her tongue and looked back out to sea.

'Just saying,' said Kelly, 'a shame to waste such a great place.'

'I'm with someone, thank you very much.'

'Oh, yes. So you said. Tell me about him, then.'

So Nancy described Leo Rooney, in looks and character. Kelly drank her smoothie, then did start to admire Nancy's chest.

'So, let me get this right,' said Kelly. 'If this Leo hopped off a beached speedboat right here and now, it would be just the hottest sight imaginable?'

Nancy could not help but smile. For just a fraction of a second she looked up, hoping it might just be happening, but all she saw were empty waves coming in. The memory of Leo's torso above her made her giggle. Kelly laughed too. The girls moved closer in the water. Memories and thoughts were silently shared, the perfect temperature, the breeze, the pool, Kelly trying to rub nipples, Nancy pulling away. Then the moment passed. Nancy messed with her hair, looked out to sea, and then thought about finding her bikini top.

That night, they dined al fresco on the patio, under the gas lights. The best cutlery and glasses had been brought out by the two girls, and everyone had made the effort to dress up. Lots of alcohol was being consumed and the conversations were quickly on the bawdy side. Kelly had come up with garlic prawn balls for starters, before

Nancy helped Eddi serve up the pizza he had been slaving over.

Kelly sat with Francesco, who was continually messing with the top knot she had insisted he keep in all day. Ryan had shaved and moisturised to within an inch of his life, and sat there looking extremely buff, in a crisp, white shirt, open to the navel. Michael was all in designer black. Nancy found herself looking at him the most, for some reason she could not put her finger on. Only Tommy let the side down, wearing shirt and trousers, but also a baseball cap, low to his eyes, as he said he was suffering from heatstroke.

Through a mouthful of pizza, Tommy was telling a story to Ryan. Nancy just caught the bit where he said, "...jeez, like a hosepipe of fanny juice..."

Michael poured more wine. Eddi joined them with his own meal. Francesco had a hand on his own chest, inside his shirt, as he tried to convince Kelly that whatever he had just whispered into her ear was true. Nancy drank deeply of her wine. When she saw Eddi smiling at her, she patted his thigh.

'Ain't this nice,' said Michael.

'Nowhere better I can think to be,' agreed Ryan.

Francesco lifted his glass. 'Chin chin.'

That made everyone laugh. Afterwards, Nancy calmed herself down first, as usual, and she was getting tired of doing that. She watched Francesco. She wanted to have her hand on the back of his neck, as Kelly had right then. So, Nancy thought, she was in a bizarre game, but she still had history and feelings for these people, good and bad, and she was only human. She was just a girl. Maybe she could begin to enjoy being there?

'Eddi, mate,' said Tommy, 'this pizza tastes like fucking Ebola.'

22

Nancy was seventeen years old, and had just split up with Jason Ikin, following a tempestuous twelve months together – her first true love. The last thing she wanted to do was to go away on a family holiday to visit her mother's relatives in Indonesia. She just wanted to cry, and grieve, perhaps think about taking him back, and cry some more. She had been the one to end the relationship with the philandering, but cute bastard, Jason, snogging that slapper, Keira Wainfleet, was one thing, but sleeping with her best friend, Alison...

Her beloved father talked her round, making sense about how the trip would take her mind off it all, that when she came back she would be going to college, anyway. It was a fresh start. It would be her first time there as an adult, and she would regret not going because of some moronic, apprentice builder with bad acne on his greasy forehead (Daddy never liked the boy).

So they flew Emirates Airlines out of Heathrow, via Abu Dhabi, into Soekarno-Hatta airport in Jakarta, where they were met by a conservative estimate of up to forty family members. A convoy of cars took them to a house in the Depok region. Nancy had been astonished by the madness on the roads, and the number of motorbikes, in particular, especially the ones with adults wearing crash helmets but their little children bare-headed.

They were settled in and fed superbly well; rice, chicken, lamb skewers, a variety of little local dishes Nancy particularly liking something vegetarian wrapped in thin bamboo, as well as the squid in curry sauce. Yet more relatives came to see them. The first couple of days were a whirl to Nancy, so it was a good job they were there for more than two weeks, although the humidity had been a shock, far beyond what her mother had warned about.

She and her sister, Lucy, were sharing a bedroom with a cousin called Zahira, a lovely girl, and thankfully it was air-conditioned. The mosquito plague was insane, but at least Nancy felt that her brain was her own again.

These three girls escaped the family one day, heading to the Grand Indonesia mall in the city. After a great morning's shopping, they ended up in a McDonald's restaurant. It wasn't until after the meal that Zahira realised one of the three boys in the next booth was a school friend. So, the groups merged, and Nancy found herself talking with just the sweetest, most adorable Indonesian boy ever, by the name of Eddi. She got the sense that normally he would have been very shy talking to a girl, but maybe the novelty of coming from London brought him out of his shell. They got on like a house on fire. There was attraction on both sides. After exhausting the topic of England, she found out that he was a trainee chef. She loved the way his eyes lit up as he described his plans for the future. Quite frankly, Nancy wanted to never leave his side ever again.

The girls had to go home, but Zahira assured Nancy that she knew Eddi well, so it would not be a flash in the pan romance with a tragic separation (Zahira read a lot of YA romance books). Indeed, the next family gathering had Eddi invited, and he turned up, all groomed and wearing his crispest white shirt, with a present of flowers for her. He was as polite as possible in taking part in the family stuff, even talking Premier League football with Nancy's approving father, but they did manage to slip away, and it was in the porch that they had their first kiss. Long, wonderful, her tongue slipping in first. He became aroused against her and was so embarrassed by it that she nearly cried with joy.

From then on, Nancy spent as much of the holiday as possible with Eddi and, when a part of the family went on the long train journey to Bali, he was invited along. That gave them some freedom. They could wander about, hand in hand, take to the water, eat wonderful seafood. On the second night, alone in the room Eddi was sharing with one of Nancy's male cousins, their kissing went much further. He fondled her under her tee-shirt, delighted with her pert, little breasts, and she went into his pants. It got hot and steamy. Being the experienced one, Nancy wanted to make love, but he wasn't ready. Oh, she sighed happily, if he got any sweeter then she would just die, she knew it. She kissed him and told him it was all right. Instead, right there and then, she slowly knelt, giving him her best doe eyes, and went down on him.

Back home in England, the separation was intolerable, despite texting and using Skype as often as possible. Desperate plans were made for him to fly over. A visa was applied for, a letter of support written by Nancy's father, and he finally arrived four months later, with emotional scenes in Heathrow airport.

He was given his own bedroom for his ten day stay, Nancy not expecting him to be allowed into her room. As soon as they could, they found privacy and made out. It was a big issue for him that he still felt unsure about making love, but she assured him that it was of no consequence, that she just wanted him there, and they could play a bit, anyway. She performed oral sex, and he had no qualms about returning the compliment. They showered together, they desperately embraced and kissed, held hands, they were inseparable, just not taking the final step.

He was shown around London's tourist attractions, especially enjoying the Tower. He wanted to be where Anne Boleyn had been executed. Nancy's extended family, including Nana, put on a big meal in his honour, and he and Nancy took a few day trips out. Overall, he fell in love with England and was determined to come to live there one day.

Once he was back in Indonesia, they continued the correspondence, but it became harder and harder. Nancy had her new world of college, new friends, new admirers. Eddi would always be her beautiful, steadfast, wonderful love from Jakarta, but life overtook them. Nancy was no angel; she had desires, and wanted as much fun as the next English girl. Then, she was introduced to a young, cheeky lad called Tommy, who was funny, sexy, persistent, available, and not 8,000 miles away.

23

Another day in paradise started for Nancy by walking barefoot across the lawn, sipping a cup of tea, while watching Ryan and Michael throwing a baseball back and forth. The tea caused her to remember the attempts she had made to send Tetley tea to one of her cousins in Jakarta – no package ever made it. She smiled.

Both Americans were shirtless, just in black shorts and their baseball caps, the ball smacking into their leather gloves with loud slaps. The two men watched her approach, and she was about to ignore them, head off to look out over the ocean, when Michael addressed her.

'You liked our trip to Yankee stadium, didn't you, Nancy?'

'Yes, Michael, I liked it. I didn't understand anything that was going on, but I liked it.'

Ryan put in a stronger throw, making his rib cage expand, much to Nancy's liking, despite herself.

'Nancy, you should have come out ten minutes earlier,' Ryan told her. 'We were comparing your technique.'

She curled the right side of her top lip. 'How very charming.'

The two men quit their game. Standing between them, as she was, Nancy imagined a wild threesome, briefly, until forcing the idea from her mind. Instead, she asked them what they had been up to recently. Michael decided to sit on the grass, so they followed suit, and Ryan described the Roman, soft-porn movie shoot in California. Nancy's eyes went wide, jealous of that production assistant girl who had squatted down in the bath house. Then Michael told them about his vacation to the Isle of Man TT races, and of his friend somersaulting into a field of cows. Nancy could not help but snigger.

'I remember your bike, Michael,' she said. 'You wouldn't let me sit on it.'

'I let you sit on everything else, baby.'

Ryan laughed at that. Nancy brushed her hair back, nervously keeping the mug of tea covering her bare abdomen, as she felt Michael's eyes bore into her. That threesome image invaded her thoughts again, with her on her hands and knees on her bed, being taken from behind by Michael, as deep as possible, as Ryan pushed his cock into her mouth. Those amazing manhoods. She actually tried to visualise them; Ryan's long and smooth, Michael's more veiny, more angry. God, she thought, and was about to get up and leave, when Ryan touched her knee to get her attention.

'So, Nancy, who did you prefer between the two of us?'

She dug up her dirtiest look for Ryan lowering the tone again. 'Michael, of course.'

Michael laughed.

'Why did you leave him for me, then?'

Michael stopped laughing. His eyes were cold, and he exuded a menacing demeanour with his dark growth of beard.

'Now, now, boys,' said Nancy, 'behave yourselves. Carry on with your game, you need to tone up a fraction more.'

She walked away. In front of her, Tommy and Kelly sauntered out into the sun and, to Nancy's surprise, they seemed to be talking about spanking.

'Yeah, there was this bird called Elizabeth,' said Tommy. 'Her arse was like Willy Wonka's everlasting gobstopper.'

'It was like *what!?*' asked Kelly, incredulous.

'No matter how much I spanked it, it never got sore.'

Kelly screamed with laughter.

Nancy had drifted away, but found Ryan following close on her heels.

'Yes, Ryan?'

'I was thinking of going snorkelling. I wondered if you would like to join me?'

'Errrm, sure, why not?'

'Good, I'll meet you on the beach in, what, ten?'

'Ten minutes, okay.'

So, Nancy went upstairs to change. She gave consideration to all her bikinis, settling on the tiniest one. As she adjusted the top half, worried about her nipples showing through, Leo Rooney did cross her mind, but she blinked hard, moved away from the mirror in shame, then leant back in to check hair, and skipped down and out through the front door.

Ryan waited out in the morning glare, carrying goggles and flippers for both of them, plus one nasty-looking spear gun. Naturally, he ogled Nancy all the way across the sand to him, then led her to the area of the bay he had already decided on. As they chatted about nothing in particular, Nancy realised that she was just savouring... something... about Ryan, something that she presumed must be pheromones or the like, being so close to his, toned, fat-free, buff body, with his slight, fair newly-grown beard and those pure white teeth.

Anyway, they were sitting on the sand, putting on their flippers. The surf was calm, but Nancy could still hear it, placing her for a moment into the *From Here To Eternity* beach scene, considering how it would feel for Ryan's torso to press her forcibly into the sand while kissing her hard with his open mouth. Then he was hauling her to her feet, telling her they would not be not be going too far offshore, taking her hand again, once her goggles were on top of her head. They clown-walked out into the sea, and Nancy thought the water was heavenly. Then Ryan managed to tell her that he was really pleased to have the chance to know her again. Nancy smiled at him, but concentrated on the snorkelling ahead.

What followed was a fun hour and a half, or so, of playing about in the sea, starting with Ryan's guiding hands on Nancy's thighs and belly as she took a while to reacquaint herself with the activity. She fell off him, deliberately, three or four times. There was lots of embracing, laughing, wet hair tossing, and some decent snorkelling. Nancy laughed. She could feel the sun on all the water droplets clinging to her body. If the good life was just snorkelling in the Caribbean, then Ryan was the perfect guy for it.

The weather had changed by the time they were having "tea", with squally rain moving in, prompting them to all eat indoors. Nobody had bothered to cook a communal meal, so they were eating a variety of separate things. Everybody except Eddi was drinking red wine.

'It doesn't rain constantly in England,' responded Kelly to a jibe from Francesco.

Nancy saw that those two were getting pretty close. Some kind of relationship was bound to develop between her Exes, so it might as well be them. Nearby, Michael and Ryan were talking about some political elections coming up, back home in the States. Eddi, on the sofa beside her, was making complimentary noises about the tuna sandwich she had made him. Tommy, propped on a stool, wearing a white vestlet and pale pink shorts, finished eating soup, before pointing his spoon at Francesco.

'Went to Florence once to watch Chelsea play Fiorentina,' he said. 'It rained the whole fucking time.'

'Then we must have rain, too,' replied Francesco.

'It was raining when I left London,' said Kelly.

Tommy went over to put his bowl in the sink. 'Maybe we need to start collecting rainwater, if we're here for life. Hey, Michael, are you talking politics? Write to your Senator and beg to be rescued.'

'Write to your MP,' replied Michael.

Tommy laughed. 'Don't get me started on British MPs. Fucking hell. Bent bastards, the lot of them. What happened to my fucking tax credits? That's what I want to know. I'll tell you what sums up MPs, apart from their perversions and greed. There was this MP, in charge of transport policy, popped up on TV one day, telling drivers not to hog the middle lane of the motorway at 70mph. To move over for other traffic. What other traffic!? The speed limit is seventy, and this Public School fuckwit is telling people to get out of the way of speeders. Mind you, you have some right big scandals in American politics, don't you?' Tommy sat on the arm of a sofa near to Ryan, shaking his head. 'America. America. What a place that is. What is it, ninety per cent of Americans don't have passports and have no plans to ever leave the country? Isn't that somewhat backward?' Ryan looked sideways at Tommy, who continued. 'Backwards, eh, Ryan? And don't get me started on American girls. What sums up American girls to me are those *Youtube* examples of cheerleaders running to rearrange banners at football games, and then getting flattened as the whole football team comes storming through it.' He laughed manically. 'Fucking stupid American bitches.' He sighed deeply. 'So, got any sisters, Ryan?'

Ryan was on his feet in a flash, joined a fraction later by Tommy, so it was Ryan who got off the first punch. Nancy heard the blow land, just like in the movies, connecting with Tommy's suddenly furious face. Then there was pandemonium, Kelly screaming, Tommy punching back, Francesco trying to break them up, Ryan really going at it with both fists, Michael finally pulling his man back onto a sofa and restraining him. Somehow, Tommy's vest had been ripped, so he tore it from his body in a rage, blood streaming from his mouth. Francesco pulled the Englishman clear.

Nancy sighed back and pulled her hair up tight. Then she held the arm of an unmoved Eddi beside her. She should have been like her mum, and stuck with one man for life.

24

Nancy woke up on her front, slightly agitated and sweating on her forehead from a mad dream, the contents of which she happily allowed to slip away into a dark recess of her mind. She breathed deeply of the sea air and grinned as she imagined being on top of Leo in New York, tracing a finger around his chest tattoo, up under his neck, enjoying his satisfied purrs, moving up to kiss his stubbly chin. Asking to shave him and being strongly rebuffed. How she wanted to curl her little hand around his shaft and feel it grow big. She could go down there and kiss his rock hard abdomen, get a close-up view of her actions.

'Aaargh!' She rolled over in mild frustration. Time to get up and see if she was still marooned with four vain hunks, one bi-sexual harlot, and one adorable Indonesian. She hit the shower first. While shampooing her hair, she remembered that it was her turn on the rota to cook that evening's meal, so gave some thought to that, although cooking was not her forté. Oh, well, they would get what they were given and be happy with it.

She decided to sit on her balcony to dry her hair, before going downstairs. Not a soul was about, with no human sound, prompting her towards paranoid thoughts of everybody having been removed from the island during the night, to leave her to go on alone, until she starved. Then, from the position of the sun, she guessed that she had woken very early. She decided to go down, make a cup of tea, and return to the glorious balcony, which she did without encountering any house mates. Back in position, she started thinking about Michael, for some reason.

She had met Michael in a roundabout, blink and you miss him, kind of way. Viewing a property in Battery Park, the seller's neighbour had been training for a triathlon, together with his friend, who happened to be Michael. Looking at the outside space had coincided with the two men getting back from a long cycle ride, exhausted and joking over the fence with Nancy's client about the joy of triathlon. Nancy appraised the two super fit men, especially Michael, who had looked at her while the two neighbours continued to chat. Nancy would have given it no more thought, until quickly blended smoothies had been offered over as continuation of the discussion. Nancy happily tried her drink, told Michael she felt instantly fitter. He had flattered her by saying she was fit enough already, which led to conversation, numbers exchanged, and a date five days later.

He took her to Buddakan, the Asian fusion place in Chelsea. Of course, he knew what her occupation was, so told her all about his modelling ambitions. Indonesia was explained and he was very interested in everything to do with Asia. All in all, they had a very pleasant evening. Nancy fancied the man enormously, though there wasn't an instant connection there. Although confident within herself, she had not been in New York very long, so perhaps felt nervous about her first romantic entanglement.

They went for a drink, then he got her home. There was a gentlemanly kiss, and that was it. All normal. All good. They met again in the week, for a casual lunch, where he offered to take her out on his motorbike that coming weekend. Secretly, she wasn't too keen, but, as it was his great passion in life, she agreed and they rode out into the countryside on Sunday. She was surprised how excited she got being behind him, holding him round his rock hard waist. The day turned out to be fun. They stopped at a diner. There were gentle kisses. Afterwards, he took her back to his *pied-a-terre* on the Upper East Side, for when he was in the city. He fed her, then seduced her. Through to the bedroom, he proceeded to have her quite roughly, ripping her panties from her body, pinning her down, some hair pulling, deep French kissing, lifting her as easily as a rag doll. It was new for her to be taken so forcefully, disconcerting, but also extremely exciting. He licked her pussy like a madman, all the while with his hands clamped on her boobs. Then he rose up and she was faced with the biggest mouthful she had ever seen. She dealt with it as best she could, despite his controlling hands in her hair.

The lovemaking started with caresses and whispered words, but once he was in her there followed such an aggressive banging that she was spent and sweating afterwards. He was draped on her, breathing heavily, saying things about needing her desperately, and that it wouldn't be so nasty next time. Not that she was complaining, having come twice, but, yes, he had been a little bit frightening.

It was while dating Michael that Nancy first met Ryan. It was before his relocation to Hollywood, when he was just a courier, needing to make occasional visits into the Crow East office. Zach spotted him first, once even making a special trip to the water cooler just to be near the door when the man left. Nancy had cause to speak to him on a few occasions, finding him not too bright, a little arrogant, perhaps already dreaming of doing something more worthy. He was, however, extremely easy on the eye. And that was that, seeing as she was attached.

She was settled into the relationship with Michael. She was busy learning the market; he was often away on photo shoots, so they were not exactly in each other's pockets. Life revolved around getting together whenever they could, eating out, then having rough sex, interspersed with watching him work on his motorbike, or work on his fitness. He never asked about her family, so she didn't ask about his. After about two months, she realised that the only thing they had in common was sex. So when that hunky courier spent thirty minutes in her company one day, while an address mistake was rectified, she had no qualms about getting to know him better. Yes, he only spoke about himself, about his acting lessons, his plans to relocate, but it was a refreshing change for Nancy; not too intense.

But then she met Michael, that evening, and he'd had a disappointment, failing to get a major modelling assignment, so he was in a surly mood, not wanting to go out. He hit the whiskey bottle. Finally, after an uncomfortable evening, he joined Nancy in the shower, forced her up against the wall, and spanked her hard.

Again, Nancy was not unwilling, just a little taken aback. But to be then marched to the bed still soaking wet, to be roughly taken from behind, while still being spanked like a horse, and called filthy names, her hair yanked painfully, pulling her chin up. Then she realised he was dribbling saliva into her asshole, holding his big cock at the ready. Without any more preamble, he went ahead and did what he wanted to do to her.

Ryan asked her out, the next time he came into the office. She thought of him as a harmless puppy asking for a biscuit. If there hadn't been any Michael on the scene, she would have agreed, but she politely put him off. He was surprised (being refused was not something he was used to) but stayed friendly and made sure to say goodbye when his package had been received by the agent, down the hall.

Nancy kept thinking about the blond courier guy, even while out on the town in Michael's Range Rover that evening. Michael's agent had coerced him into taking a job which he didn't like the sound of, so he was quiet again, giving Nancy the minimum of conversation. Nancy knew better than to bother him, just watching the world go by, looking forward to her tea, and the passionate sex afterwards.

Suddenly, there was a loud bang. Nancy jumped out of her skin, thinking someone was shooting at them, but then she realised that a cyclist had ridden into the side of the car. They were stationary at traffic lights, and the cyclist was standing there with a buckled front wheel in his hands. She shot a look at Michael, but he was just putting the vehicle into neutral, not looking out at the cyclist, not even swearing. He slowly got out and assessed the damage to his side of the vehicle. Nancy watched him begin conversation with the cyclist, a man of about forty years of age. It all seemed amicable, no raised voices, no gesticulating about rights of way. She just started to think of her tea being delayed, feeling quite petulant, wondering if Michael would bother trying to get details from the man for insurance purposes. Completely out of nowhere, she witnessed Michael suddenly grab the cyclist by the head, pull him in and then clamp his teeth on the man's nose. When the shocked cyclist managed to shake himself free, he had blood pouring from the bite mark on his nose. He stumbled backwards onto his broken bike, ashen-faced, looking like he had been attacked by a zombie. Michael climbed calmly into the Range Rover and drove them away.

Nancy said not a word about what she had seen; she was too disturbed, so she went to the restaurant with him, ate her tea, listened to him try to talk himself into being okay with the job his agent wanted. She went back to his apartment and let him fuck her for most of the evening, before making an excuse about an early meeting so she could leave at midnight. Then, however best she could do it, she determined to be done with the man for good.

25

Kelly and Francesco were sleeping together, which kind of changed the mood in the villa. Everyone pretended that it didn't bother them, but it was there, in slightly longer pauses between conversation, with more care taken in choosing where to sit near to them, and trying to give them space when they couldn't take their eyes off each other.

Francesco had decided to cook everyone pasta for lunch, so he was there in the kitchen, flamboyantly banging pots and pans around, with Kelly watching on, coquettishly amused. Nancy looked at them for a while, then saw that Ryan was becoming restless. There was only so many times he could arrange his hair to take his mind off the Anglo-Italian love-fest.

'Shall we take a walk?' she suggested.

In getting up, his thin vest revealed the straining of his rib cage to Nancy. She gave some consideration to asking him to wear proper tee-shirts, to remove temptation, then they were flip-flopping down around the pool and the tennis courts, talking of nothing much. It was overcast, electricity in the air, which gave

Nancy pleasure through the hairs on the nape of her neck.

'I was talking to Tommy this morning,' said Ryan. 'He said, if he doesn't get laid soon, he's going to throw himself off the roof.'

'Oh, did he? Looks like he's a bit short of options, at the moment. You could volunteer, I suppose.'

They both laughed. They had wandered to the far right side of the grounds, and could hear the other boys on the go-carts.

'Maybe we should go tell them to come back for lunch,' suggested Ryan.

Nancy indicated the Love Nest, right above them. 'In a bit. Let's sit up there and chill for a few minutes. Anyway, the storm is coming, so they'll come running back.'

They climbed up the spiral staircase and reclined on the sofas, looking out over what was quite a turbulent sea and dark horizon.

'What about you?' she asked. 'On the getting laid front?'

'Me? I've got more self-control than Tommy.'

They looked at each other; his black top seemed to be of a similar material to her casual black dress. While she seemed slightly darker since arriving, he was still pale, apart from a touch of redness to the nose.

'Beautiful island,' he said, looking back out to sea. 'But I wouldn't come to this kind of place normally. How much longer do you think we'll be here?'

That question triggered an emotional response from Nancy, tears springing into her eyes.

'Hey, hey!' he said, pulling her into an embrace. 'Something will develop soon. I'm sure of it.'

She wept while he held on to her. Finally, she sat up and wiped her eyes.

'It's to be expected,' he said. 'You've been pretty strong, so far.'

She blew out her cheeks, gaining control. 'I don't normally cry. My sister is the one who cries. I'm the tough one. I'm the one who moved to New York, after all. I make the big commission. I've made mistakes, I'm not perfect, some people dislike me, some people are jealous of my pretty face, jealous that I can have men like you. But what did I do to deserve all this?'

Ryan didn't know what to say, so stroked her hair.

'Ryan, do you think I'm a bad person?'

'Not at all, no.'

'Sometimes, I don't think I'm very nice, you know. I'm selfish. Spoilt and selfish. I've used people most of my life. I pretend that they've used me, but it's not true. Maybe I think I'm better than anyone else.'

Ryan's limited brain cells were into overdrive. 'Hey, you're normal. You have to live your life as best you can. Sometimes you get hurt, sometimes you hurt people. Don't fret on it.'

She thrust her hands up through her hair, as she tended to do when frustrated.

'I treated Eddi appallingly, just because he was too far away for my lazy head to deal with. I left things badly with Kelly, because she was a girl. I messed with Francesco's head but was too childish to carry through with him. I ran away from Tommy as soon as New York came along, although he was an annoying prick. I left Michael for you, even though he was another annoying prick. And I drove you away from me to the other side of the country.'

'That's nonsense. You always knew I was going.'

'But if I had treated you right, you wouldn't have wanted to go. If I was more giving. More generous. So, I'm this grasping, unpleasant... *thing* from London who nobody likes in the end. I don't deserve happiness.'

Ryan's counselling abilities seemed exhausted, so he looked happy when the sky suddenly blackened and torrential rain began to fall. They decided to make a run for the villa, and were joined by Michael, Tommy and Eddi for the last few feet into the kitchen. Nancy hugged Eddi, cheered to see him. She shook the rain from her hair.

'So, do you love the go-carts, Eddi?'

'They are great fun, Nancy.'

'Shall we do luncheon?'

'Yes, let's.'

Francesco's pasta, which went down much better than Eddi's burgers, made Nancy look back to her single season in Madesimo, where she worked as a chalet maid. The actual, tedious, dirty work could easily be expunged from her memory, but the town held a special charm for her; she had made some nice friends, the skiing was fantastic, and she met the four Mazza brothers. She had wanted Nino, but he was in love with a local girl at the time. Younger Francesco had worked his silver-tongued magic on her, so, in the end, all her spare time had been spent either in his bed, or in his care while off-piste, high in the mountains.

At school, Nancy had shown an interest in German, Spanish and Italian. Having once visited Rome with the family, she had a leaning towards Italy when a friend suggested making a little money for a few months. Now she thought about it, sitting there in the villa, she had let a lot of the Italian experience pass her by. It had all been so fast, so expected; the occasional skiing, the pizza, the wine, the getting up late for work, the flirting from holidaying men behind their wives' backs, then the relationship with Francesco. Yes, he had smooth-talked her, yes, it had been fun, the sex amazing, but why had she not savoured it more? Again, she reproached herself, but then put it down to being young. She supposed every youngster lived through great times without appreciating them fully. Or was she being sentimental? Francesco's eye had always been roving around the pretty holidaymakers. He had probably cheated on her. Best to leave Madesimo in its box as a fun little working holiday with some local added flavour.

It made her compare Francesco's right to be there on the island, while Jason Ikin was not. What was wrong with Jason? Had he refused to come? Surely the money would have tempted him. She desperately hoped he wasn't unwell. There had been two other men: flings, who definitely deserved no place on that Caribbean freak show.

There was chocolate dessert, brought over to her by Eddi. He asked if she was all right, and she smiled at him.

'Great lunch,' he said. 'He should be a chef.'

'Eddi, let's do something together this afternoon.'

He hesitated. 'Er, would you like to go on the go-carts? We planned to return as soon as the rain stopped.'

She laughed. 'Oh, my adorable Eddi. You go back to your little toys, my sweet boy.'

He grinned. 'What will you do?'

'Oh, Kelly brought a few paperbacks, by people I've never heard of, but never mind. I'll just sit and read, while waiting for you to drive up through the trees. We'll see if the noise upsets my perfect vacation.'

In the end, it was Tommy who disturbed her reading. Nancy was sprawled out on a shaded, dry mound of earth. Every time Tommy circled past, he said something inappropriate. She just glared at him, then smiled and waved at Eddi, before ignoring Michael on his circuit. But Tommy, she remembered, had not been so childish when they had dated. Always game for a laugh, occasionally sulky when he didn't get his way, but it was only on the island that there had been this silliness coming from him. She presumed he had stored up resentment since she ended things suddenly, when her dream job came along. Perhaps it was a male pride thing. How dare a woman leave him!? But then, again, she wondered if she had just missed his terrible character traits. Had all her relationships been based on looks, Jager bombs, nice clothes and holidays? She sighed back, trying not to be so hard on herself. But what of Leo? Wasn't that all based on appearance and lifestyle? Where was the true love? Where was that exciting, non-sexual tingle that she had when she thought Jason was about to come round or simply telephone? That perfect joy of real love? Where was Leo Rooney in her hour of need? Why was he not rushing down to rescue her? Aside from the fact that she was still within her scheduled vacation time, that was.

Still, she was grumpy, and, after waving once more to Eddi, she got up and set off back to the villa.

26

Emerging through the trees, Nancy found Ryan sitting under the Love Nest, whittling away at a large piece of wood with a kitchen knife. 'Ryan, what on *earth* are you doing?'

'Hi, babe. I'm making a baseball bat.'

'Oh, no shit? A baseball bat? Fine.'

She carried on walking, until faced with a giggling Kelly being chased outside by Francesco, who was carrying armfuls of soap suds the washing-up had clearly degenerated into horseplay. Nancy turned on her heels and ascended into the Love Nest to continue her reading, saying to Ryan, 'Come and do your... whittling up here, in comfort.'

The two of them settled down on the sofa, each to their own pastime. Occasionally, Nancy watched the rain clouds drift further away across the sky, or glanced at Ryan, whittling his wood, which wasn't as annoying as she had feared.

'Do you mind if I take my shirt off?' he asked.

After the storm, the humidity had suddenly built up.

'No, I don't mind.'

Nancy was getting to a raunchy part of her book, so, adding that to now having a topless whittler next to her, she became a little hot and bothered herself. She thought it best to put the book down.

'Coconuts,' she suddenly said to Ryan, startling him. 'Maybe we should start collecting coconuts for sustenance.'

Ryan tossed his blond hair from his eyes. 'Have we got to that stage yet?'

'Kelly's in charge of supplies. I'll ask her when I go down.'

He looked a little disappointed. 'Are you going down?'

'Do you want me to go down?'

'Huh?'

'I mean, do you want some privacy?'

'No, not really.'

'I'll stay, then.'

'Okay.'

'Are you having fun? Whittling? Is it for you and Michael?'

'No, I thought everyone could have a game, on the beach. We could use coconuts as bases.'

Nancy laughed, dropping onto his shoulder without thinking, and then staying there. He was pleased with his witty remark.

'You know, Nancy, when we were together, I didn't find you in any way like you were saying before. Do you understand?' She rubbed her chin up and down on his shoulder by way of response. 'Good. No need to be down on yourself. We're all complicated and stuff.'

Obviously out of his comfort zone in offering counselling, Ryan reverted to what he knew best, and that was having a gorgeous woman being in contact with his hard body. He started to stroke

Nancy's hair, and allowed his fingertips to linger softly around her left ear. It was intoxicating to Nancy, dreamy, arousing, until Leo Rooney flashed up in her brain, causing her to sit up.

'Hey, hey,' whispered Ryan. 'We're not doing anything wrong.'

'But we are. And yet still you are touching my neck.'

'It's so smooth, Nancy. Just like I remember. Silk. I need to kiss it.'

'Ryan, please.'

'Your man's not here. I am.'

'Shush.' She tapped her right temple. 'He's in here.'

But Ryan was already lowering his mouth, to send her near to ecstasy with his lips tracing up and down her slender neck. She mumbled something in the negative, but delighted in his hand moving to her left breast, squeezing, finding the excited nipple.

'No, no, no,' she said, pulling away. 'I can't have sex while I'm here. That's just... wrong. On so many levels.'

'Let's just play, then,' he suggested, closing the gap again.

She glanced at his obvious arousal through his shorts. 'I'm not even touching that, so don't even think about it.'

'Let me massage you, Nancy.'

'Just a massage?'

'Uh-huh.'

'Well... it can't hurt, I suppose.'

'No, it can't hurt. You know I'm the best at it.'

'Oh, like I've never heard that before. I don't know, Ryan, maybe I should just go back into the villa.'

'And do what? Come on, I promise not to do anything bad. I won't put anything in you.'

'Ryan! Do you have to talk like that?'

He was fondling her waist. 'I won't put anything in you that you tell me not to put in you.'

Nancy sighed and pushed her hair up once more. All kinds of things flashed through her mind: the lovely location, Ryan's wonderful man smell, the warm Caribbean breeze flowing across them, Gabby, back in New York, telling her that Leo would have someone else in his bed by then, Ryan's hand taking charge of her slender side.

'God, Ryan. Like I said earlier, I'm not an angel. I'm so horny for you right now. But just a massage, right? You will not attempt to put your dick in me.' Ryan grinned and licked his lips. 'Or your tongue. You swear?'

'I swear. No dick or tongue. Now get comfortable. Take that dress off.'

'I'm sorry!?'

'I can't do a proper massage through it. Look, I'll turn away until you are lying on the couch.'

Nancy eyeballed the taut muscles of Ryan's back, before slipping the dress over her head, and lying flat out in just her panties. Next thing she knew, after a pause where he must have appraised her near nudity, she felt his hands beginning their work at her shoulders, and it was obvious how tense she had been holding herself on the island. He made her moan immediately. He had straddled her, sitting his groin down on her bottom. His fingers got into her tissue, and he took his time; they had all the time in the world, after all.

'Good?' he asked.

'Oh, good.'

'You remember, don't you, my massage technique?'

'I remember. Barely top five.'

'Holy... always with the jokes.'

Gradually he moved lower, his face a picture of concentration, aware that her mouth was open in one long expulsion of pleasure. He used his thumbs, and the heel of his hands; he did a few of the karate chops, which had her laughing. Then he was picking at the waistband to her panties.

'Ryan,' she warned.

He ignored her, whipping the panties down her legs. Oh my God, she mimed. Never, ever, did she think she would be naked with Ryan again, and... there it was, his fingers kneading her buttocks. Unbelievable, turning her on massively. She felt such a mixture of excitement and guilt.

'Oh, God,' she said, as he was massaging slightly on the inside of her cheeks.

'Shall I go on to your legs now?' he asked. 'Or stay here?'

'Stay there.'

'Lift up.'

'Ryan, no. Don't get me angry.'

'No dick, no tongue.'

He lifted her bum into the air, then resumed his massage, going with great sweeps up her sleek back, then back down to firmly handle her rear.

Nancy was soaking wet, desperate for him, but still trying to make herself sit up and get dressed. Then he touched her between her legs, and her thighs opened automatically for him. He rubbed her, ever so gently. Nancy was gone in the head, by then.

'Nancy, there's something I never got to do.'

Jesus, her delirious brain mumbled to herself, why do men carry the past with them? She managed a look back at Ryan. He was sweating (the man could never survive Jakarta's temperature). She gave her best quizzical look, but he just stared back, before starting to caress up and down both of her thighs.

'What, possibly, did you not get to do?' she gasped.

His blue eyes locked with hers as he dribbled spit into her bottom.

'Oh, Christ,' she moaned.

Ryan inserted two fingers from one hand into her ass, and then two fingers from the other hand into her pussy. Nancy felt herself gush. He began to piston his fingers in and out, in turn, getting a rhythm going. Nancy started to bite the sofa. The only thing that could form in her mind were swear words to describe the pleasure and excitement.

Suddenly, from inside the villa, a male voice shouted, 'Helicopter!'

27

The helicopter passed slowly across the sky, directly above the villa. It was a small two-seater, not the red one which had brought Nancy to the island. Everyone ran out onto the lawn from wherever they had been, waving their arms and shouting. Nancy watched it go, while still trying to rearrange her panties under her dress. She looked around at everyone's faces, mostly a little shocked, while Francesco seemed exasperated.

'Is it landing?' asked Kelly.

'I'll go and see,' volunteered Eddi, running off through the villa, in the direction of the beach.

Nancy looked about her again. Ryan acted like he had been caught with his fingers in the cookie jar, arriving a little behind Nancy for the big scene. Michael appeared to be quite calm. Then she realised that Tommy was not there. She gave that no more thought as everyone decided to follow along after Eddi.

The helicopter had not landed, at least not on their beach helipad. Eddi came back to them, looking dejected. Nancy embraced him.

'A cup of tea,' suggested Kelly. 'Nothing more we can do right now.'

Nancy helped Kelly brew up, and while together in the kitchen they discussed the provisions, with Kelly estimating they would have to go on rations within a few days if nothing developed.

So, they all relaxed on the sofas, drinking tea, offering up ideas on why they had been overflown. Kelly finally banned all further talk of the incident. Instead, she asked whose turn it was to cook that evening. Michael spoke up, offering to cook the last of the steaks. Then he and Ryan departed for the garden, to confer over the baseball bat. Nancy watched Ryan go with sly eyes from beneath her fringe; his lazy flip-flop walk on the tiles, messing with his hair. She swallowed. She could still feel him inside her.

Late in the afternoon, the call went up for a baseball game, so everyone traipsed out to the beach, where the American boys had crafted a small baseball diamond in the sand. They had placed it in such a way that any hit landing in the surf would be deemed a home run. Everybody was excited to take part and, as teams were impossible to pick with only seven people, they just took turns in all the various positions.

Following a lot of practice throws and attempts to hit with the home-made bat (which was a long, sleek work of art, actually), some form of a game began. Kelly pitched underarm to Michael, and Eddi subsequently fetched back a wet baseball. Francesco and Tommy managed hits, but Nancy spent several hilarious minutes swinging at mid-air. Finally, she accepted that she had probably been struck out and playfully threw the bat down in a tantrum. She was asked to pitch next, also going underarm to Ryan, who seemed to deliberately pop a ball up high which Kelly managed to catch, using his glove. She screamed her delight and ran to Ryan for a celebratory hug, bringing her bare legs up around his waist.

Francesco shrugged at seeing his new girlfriend embracing another man, as he was enjoying the fun; he was next to bat, cracking the ball high to right field and running all the way around the bases before Tommy retrieved the ball. Michael gave Francesco double high fives as he jumped onto home plate.

Kelly was at bat; wiggling it high in the air, so she had clearly seen the sport at some stage. Nancy, lingering near first base, could only grin as she watched the sexy performance, hearing Ryan laugh and Tommy cackle. Michael pitched gently to her, and she cracked it back down the middle, whooping her delight as she started to run. She stuck out her tongue as she passed Nancy, then had to stop at second as Eddi threw the ball back in. Ryan received another, less exuberant hug. Francesco shrugged again, but that time his face was less masked.

Soon, it was too much exertion for Nancy and Kelly, preferring to lounge out in the sun and let the boys carry on. Michael hit a home run. Kelly whooped loudly in appreciation. 'You da man, Michael!'

'Are you trying to wind up Francesco?' asked Nancy.

'That wouldn't be hard, him being Italian.' Kelly clapped sand off her legs. 'I'm getting worried now, babe. Aren't you?'

'Worried about what? Our situation?'

'Of course. Maybe we should take a walk tomorrow? Somebody might be in another villa now, arrived on that helicopter. Or you and the Indonesian fella might have missed something.'

Nancy could not be bothered correcting her about Eddi's name again. 'Well, we'll go tomorrow, then.'

'Good. So, changing the subject, are you still determined to be loyal to your New York man? Why not have something here, while you still can? Tommy's always staring at you. What about Michael?'

Nancy looked over at Michael. Then at Ryan, again remembering the naughty thing he did to her in the Love Nest. 'I'll pass on Michael, thank you.'

Kelly laughed. 'Maybe I should have them all.'

'One after the other? Why not?'

'Or all at the same time!' Kelly's raucous laugh subsided into a grin as Tommy came near to retrieve the ball. 'You are so in good shape, Mr Tommy.'

For once, Tommy seemed taken aback. He managed a smile before jogging back.

Kelly was checking her suntan on her belly and forearms. 'Is my tan coming along?'

Nancy eyed the woman. 'You look all right.'

Kelly moved the straps of her bikini top. 'Ah. If we go for a walk tomorrow, maybe we can go topless, improve my all over tan.'

Nancy just looked back at the baseball players, just in time to see a running Michael turn his ankle and tumble head over heels in the sand. Everyone rushed to him. Kelly had the First Aid training, so after feeling for a break, and finding none, she assessed that the ankle was twisted, that Michael needed to be carried to the villa to put ice on it. Tommy and Ryan picked him up with ease, and the group headed in.

The two women did indeed go topless the following morning, as they went for their walk around the island, but not before they were out of sight of their own beach. Then they laughed as they put their backpacks on again, feeling like oddball, nudist ramblers. They were carrying lots of water and sandwiches made by Eddi, who had wanted to go with them. Nancy had hugged him, then waved at him, and at a watching Ryan, as they walked away.

There had been an interesting scene before the last goodbyes, back in the villa, where Michael was resting his swollen ankle. Nancy just caught the end of a conversation between the man and Kelly, where he seemed to be annoyed that the two girls were going for a hike to the other villas. Nancy could only deduce that he was concerned for their safety. Anyway, Kelly was unusually withdrawn, until they were well on their way.

Nancy led Kelly on the route that she and Eddi had taken previously. Kelly's mood was suddenly bright, Nancy saw, perhaps she was relieved to be away from the villa for a time. They took the opportunity to talk about normal things that girlfriends talk about, and of what they were looking forward to, once they got back to civilisation; Nancy wanted to visit her parents, while for Kelly it was a Nando's meal.

After a pause, Kelly asked Nancy about how she had met Francesco. She knew it had been in Italy while Nancy had been a chalet maid. Nancy didn't mind talking about it.

'You know it was in his town of Madesimo, yeah? Well, I arrived, all tired and sweaty from the journey, to join my friend who was already over there. She was working, so I got our room key from her to go and have a shower. When I walked in I could hear water running in the bathroom. I knew it was supposed to be just me and my friend, so I rushed in to investigate. I was faced with this obviously Italian hunk taking a shower.'

'Obviously Italian?'

'Well, at the risk of being thought racist, he had fairly long hair, silly beads round his neck, a cheesy grin and instead of hiding his thing, he kept vigorously washing it. Oh, and then he said, "Caio, bella! Come in and join me." Then he turned to proudly show off his butt. "Look at my ass, it's beautiful, no?"

They laughed as they moved off. They were not overtly checking out each other's bodies, but it was liberating to be hiking semi-nude like that. Kelly had put her hair into a French plait, while Nancy's flowed loose and wild. The sun beat down. The breeze came in off the empty sea.

Soon, they approached the first villa along the coast. There was no sign of life.

'Looks just as it did when me and Eddi came here,' said Nancy.

Kelly brushed a blade of grass from Nancy's mildly sweaty left breast, then continued on. 'No need to dress yet, then,' she called back.

The pale blue villa looked clean and tidy, almost ready to receive guests, but it was deathly quiet. Kelly opened the big, ornate front door and they walked into the coolness of the foyer. They had agreed, on failing to find any people present, that the kitchen would be checked for proof of occupancy. Nancy padded through and did just that. Everything was as before.

'No,' she simply said to Kelly, and they retraced their steps. They walked through the shade of trees, alongside the pool, before moving out into the countryside again. Nancy stopped, slipping off her rucksack in order to find a water bottle.

'Good idea,' said Kelly, doing the same.

Kelly watched Nancy slake her thirst, the large bottle held high, her body contorting and her ribs showing above her soft belly. There were some dark green leaves near her head, and a golden glow through the trees from the sun, and it was a beautiful scene. *Francesco, Ryan, Michael, Tommy, Eddi... before they all starved, so why not have Nancy, too?*

'Shall we sit and rest for a while?'

'No,' replied Nancy, eyeing Kelly through her fringe. 'Let's push on.'

Nancy needed that rest after the hour long walk to the next property, along the coast. It was a smaller, white villa, perhaps for use by a single family, or a couple. They approached along the beach, seeing nobody, and entered through the kitchen in the rear. Again, deathly quiet. Kelly found that there were no supplies. Nancy removed her backpack and flopped down onto a sofa, immediately seeking out her sandwiches and water. Kelly joined her.

'What a lovely place,' said Kelly.

Between munching, looking around, Nancy agreed. 'Yes, me and Eddi liked this place the best. More of a honeymooner's villa, than where we're staying.'

'You're right. It is very cosy.' She pushed strands of hair behind Nancy's ear, prompting a frown. 'Sorry. You're just so pretty, Nancy.' With practised speed, Kelly was against the other girl, her lips kissing her small jaw, and traversing down her neck. Feeling only a pleasant sigh from Nancy in reply, Kelly cupped a breast while kissing harder. Nancy's mouth turned. Kelly brushed away a few crumbs and then they were kissing frantically, fondling roughly.

Nancy pulled back. 'Let's not.'

Kelly didn't press the matter. Instead, she grinned, then stood with her rucksack in hand. 'I'll go and check out the Honeymoon suite. I need to pee, anyway.'

When she was alone, Nancy put on her tee-shirt. She put her sandwich wrapper and empty water bottle in her backpack. She looked around, wondering if there was anything useful to take with them. Finding nothing, she wandered into the foyer to wait for Kelly to come down. That's when she noticed the muddy footprints on the floor.

28

Nancy moved to stand over the footprints, which were not particularly messy, but were definitely footprints which moved across the tiles from the front door, heading up the stairs. When she and Eddi had visited the villa previously, she was sure the foyer had been pristinely clean. Somebody had been there recently; they must have done, to have left those marks. Nancy tried to think. The helicopter had obviously landed there, but not left any supplies or, clearly, cleaned up for possible new vacationers. But why? She moved about, racking her brains. No explanation came to her, except that something must have been delivered. Perhaps it was a somebody who had been dropped off there in the villa, who might, by then, be in the jungle, possibly monitoring their own base. That frightened her, and she convinced herself that it was the reason for the footprints. She could hear Kelly singing as she came out of a bathroom upstairs.

'Are we good to go?' called Kelly, skipping down the stairs.

Nancy gathered herself quickly. She glanced at the footprints again but decided not to mention them. 'Yes, nothing more for us here.'

Kelly did a mock sulk on seeing that Nancy was fully dressed. 'Oh, you've put your top on. Killjoy. Let me put my top on, wait a second.' She reached into her rucksack.

Nancy was already leaving. 'Come on.'

All of a sudden, Kelly had had enough adventuring for one day. So the two girls headed back towards their villa. They were tired, stopping twice to sit and rest. Nancy drank more of her water.

Getting near to their own beach, Kelly, who had been unusually quiet again, decided to talk about Francesco. 'Hey, he's been trying to get me to ask for a threesome.'

'A threesome with who?'

Kelly smiled. 'With you, silly.'

Nancy breathed deeply and stroked her hair back over her head. She wasn't even going to entertain that conversation. Actually, she could see some activity on their beach. 'What's that?'

It turned out to be Tommy and Ryan, both in just shorts and mules, preparing to take kayaks out into the surf. They paused to watch the girls approach.

'Any joy?' asked Ryan.

'Yes,' replied Kelly, then laughed. 'I meant no. Jeez, what am I thinking? So tired. What's all this, are you two making a break for it?'

'We can't take Eddi's cooking any more,' joked Tommy. 'No, babe, it's purely recreational. Come out with us.'

Nancy shook her head. 'Like Kelly said, we're tired.'

Ryan twirled his paddle above his head, making his shoulder muscles flex. Nancy felt just the slightest quiver in her belly. 'Oh, come on, Nancy,' he said, 'just round the bay.'

Kelly put down her backpack, to examine one of the kayaks. 'Where did you find these?'

'Under the villa, at the side,' answered Ryan.

Kelly made the decision for both herself and Nancy, keen to be paddled around the bay in the double kayaks. Nancy agreed to go, but quickly chose to be Tommy's passenger, rather than Ryan's.

'That's my old bird,' Tommy grinned. Then he noticed that the breeze was pressing Nancy's top fully into the curves of her breasts. 'Maybe we could wait a bit.'

Nancy pulled her top away from her body, more conscious of Ryan's eyes, than of Tommy's. 'Come on, if we're going, let's go.'

The kayaks were dragged out into the water. Both girls were assisted aboard, and soon the big biceps of the boys were paddling them out to sea. Tommy was stronger than Ryan, but with less skill, so they powered off sideways at first, allowing Nancy to look to the shore, then they were turned seaward, the wind taking her breath away; it was truly glorious out there. The sea was calm and there was no danger. Ryan paddled around to stay close to the other boat, and they headed along the shore.

'Ryan!' called Kelly, 'take us straight out to sea. We've got no food left, I'd prefer to go quickly.' She laughed hysterically.

Nancy had to laugh, looking across.

'Nancy?' called Tommy. 'Do you feel the same? Shall we end it all?'

'No, get me away from this madwoman!'

A race developed, both men paddling manically. Tommy's technique floundered, they swerved to port, then tipped over. Nancy was catapulted into the water, but came up laughing, wiping her face and pushing her hair back. Tommy swam to her, took her round the waist in a mock rescue. It was all good fun, with Ryan's craft coming about to watch the drama.

Tommy helped Nancy ashore, both laughing, though spluttering, and they collapsed on the sand, very much the *From Here To Eternity* scene. For a moment, Nancy enjoyed Tommy's firm body holding her from behind, his hand on her hip, his panting breath on her soaked neck, before she knelt up and tried to make herself look decent.

Nancy walked back up the beach, in need of her water bottle. Immediately, the hot breeze was drying her body, although her nipples were pushing through her top. That had been hot, romping with Tommy like that. She tried to tidy herself up, to forget that nonsense. Reaching her bag, she sank to her knees and pulled open the strings of the back pack. But instead of finding her water bottle, she was faced with two black handguns. Her world spun around her, the sky swirled with the sand, before she steadied herself, although vomit had risen to the back of her throat. She stared at the guns. Then she closed the bag, realising that it was Kelly's back pack, not hers.

Nancy stood up shakily, looked out to sea, where Ryan and Kelly were paddling along. Back down the beach, Tommy was taking the chance to sunbathe. Nancy picked up her own bag and, somehow, through her daze, found her way up to the villa.

In the lounge, she saw Eddi eating a sandwich. She hurried towards him, before realising that Michael was dozing on a sofa, resting his damaged ankle.

'You're back,' said Eddi, turning with a smile.

Nancy had managed to gain some composure, but she still had to remind herself to blink. She quietly asked him to join her in her room in a few minutes. Then she got a glass of water, downed it, and headed upstairs.

Nancy felt chilled to the bone. Panic and fear engulfed her as she climbed the stairs to her room. From the window on the upstairs landing, she could see Kelly and the two guys, walking in through the palm trees, with kayaks being dragged behind them in the sand. Nancy felt bullied, scared, as if evil was coming for her. She felt as if she was in an American school, with a shooter loose on the campus, but without the hope of the police showing up to rescue her. She had already calculated, that morning, that her vacation ended that day, but, with the sun starting to set, no helicopter was coming for her. She moved into her room and just stood there, shivering, trying to decide what, if anything, she could do.

Eddi knocked and entered, and immediately crossed the room as he could see her distress. 'Nancy, what's wrong? You're scaring me.'

Nancy silently took him by the hand, led him into the bathroom. She set the hot shower working, then stripped naked in front of him, despite his alarm and attempts to leave. 'No,' she said, and fumbled for his belt.

'Nancy!?' he pleaded, embarrassed.

But she had his pants open, then was pushing up at his top, before stepping back into the shower. The jet hit the back of her head and sprayed over her shoulders. 'Come in and hold me, Eddi. Please.'

Eddi lost his clothes and stepped into Nancy's embrace.

'Right, we're on rations from now on,' called Kelly, from her position in the kitchen.

Nancy sat close to Eddi on a sofa, with everyone else nearby. It was evening. Drink was being imbibed. Nancy pretended to acknowledge Kelly's statement when the woman's look came round to her she was being as normal as possible, while inside she still felt nauseous. Eddi had not been let in on the news of the guns. She had just told him that she had argued with Kelly. That was all forgotten. Although they both felt awkward about him briefly getting hard in the shower.

'We'll do some fishing,' volunteered Ryan.

Nancy looked over her wine glass at all her Exes. She examined all their faces, all except Kelly's, and wondered who she could trust. Opposite her, Francesco seemed to be in a dark mood, brooding within his long hair. Maybe he was upset at not getting that threesome he wanted. Michael seemed okay, with his ankle pain almost gone and the swelling going down. Tommy was up on his feet, drinking whiskey, playfully eyeballing Eddi, who had politely declined the challenge of a game of pool. Ryan was his normal self, preening away at his hair and beard, and then his toenails.

'I volunteer to barbecue the smallest person here,' said Tommy. 'I think that's you, Nancy.' He laughed, sitting himself down beside her and squeezing her around the shoulders. Nancy half-laughed, trying to shrug him off. 'You'll feed us for a week, I reckon,' continued Tommy. 'Quite tender meat on your bones. Oh, but then I won't be able to rescue you from the sea again.' He pulled her against him. He was being quite inappropriate. Everyone was watching.

'Get off,' Nancy said, softly.

'Come on, Nancy. Don't be like that. We're all friends here.'

'Get off!'

Both Ryan and Eddi were on their feet. Ryan spoke for them both, telling Tommy to desist with his behaviour. Tommy still had hold of Nancy. Perhaps it was a little bit of stir crazy emotion rising in him, maybe too much booze, but he seemed to be considering taking them both on.

'Tommy,' called Michael. 'Just stop.'

Tommy shrugged, laughed it off, and went to find another drink.

29

In his New York City apartment, Leo Rooney was doing his early morning ablutions, standing in his mirrored shower, washing his tattooed skin with great thoroughness, across his chest, around his neck, down his six-pack to his cock and balls, happy with his stunning appearance, as always. Not that he thought of himself as vain. He just knew he was a handsome man, who loved tattoos, and was brave enough to go all the way with them, unlike those cowards and charlatans who just had one, or managed to stretch to an arm sleeve. He turned, his hand washing across his buff, ink-free backside, liking that just as much.

After towelling down, and doing a good brushing of his white teeth, he went through to his bedroom, continuing to air dry, and gave his attention to the appropriate clothing needed for what he knew was ahead of him. He was happy with the items he had laid out on his bed. He did his hair a little in the wardrobe mirror. Once his body was completely dry, he first of all put on an elasticated medical support on his right knee, for an old basketball injury, then stepped into his first of two pairs of boxer shorts. On top of those he put on a small boxer's groin guard – small as in not bulky around the hips, not small in respect to his manhood, which he made comfortable inside. From painful experience, he just wanted protection for the crown jewels. After his second pair of underpants went on, he examined himself in the mirror. 'Sturdy,' he said to himself, and laughed. Then came heavy socks, followed by thick camo trousers, a black tee-shirt, then two heavy-duty military-style tops. He knelt by his holdall on the floor, reaching inside, happy with the equipment held within. He carried the bag to the kitchen, where he loaded it with food supplies and water from the fridge. He threw in some mints, a couple of Hershey bars, some painkillers and then zipped it closed.

He checked his watch. He was on schedule. His coffee was ready, so he poured a cup and sat down on a stool. The sun was just about to appear over a nearby building. His realised his feet were tapping with adrenalin, so keen was he to get down there, to where the action was. It wasn't often that he took that kind of trip, but he knew he would handle himself properly, that his people could rely on him, that his mind would keep functioning in the heat of the moment.

He looked at his cell phone, no more messages. Damn, that coffee was great. The moment was great, everything was great; those people didn't know who they were messing with.

He washed his coffee cup, checked around the apartment, then he was ready to go, shouldering his bag. With a repositioning of his groin, as if it were a Medieval codpiece, he locked up and went down to the garage.

Visions of Nancy Niven came to him as he drove out into the

traffic, which was understandable, really, given the circumstances. She was an adorable creature. A very sexy woman. He put the radio on. The tune was beautiful, although he struggled to name it – some man singing about being born again and asking to be comforted through all the madness.

Daniel Bridgford was trying to control his highly anxious state. The American Airlines 737 was making its final approach to Stockholm Arlanda International Airport. Alongside him were two Swedish Asian teenage boys, and there had been several nice chats throughout the flight from JFK, about Sweden, America, possible American colleges for them, and about the New England Patriots football club, although Daniel had not been much help on that one. The conversations had taken his mind off his distressing reason for the flight to Sweden: the news of his partner, Ulrika, being involved in a road traffic accident. That was the cause of his anxiety. Then the wheels touched down, which did actually help calm his nerves.

Stockholm was chilly but dry. He took a taxi, and was pleased to be seeing the Swedish capital again, despite the distressing circumstances. Ulrika's family was small and spread out to the north, so it had been a friend who had managed to contact him in New York. His girlfriend's condition was not life threatening, he was led to believe, but he needed to be with her, as soon as possible.

Not being able to pronounce the name of the hospital, Daniel had written it down before leaving home and gave that piece of paper to the taxi driver. They arrived within twenty minutes. He paid off the cab and rushed into the hospital reception.

He had to wait for what seemed an inordinate length of time, but then a hospital official, by the name of Helen, took charge of him and he was led on a long walk to the relevant ward. There he was handed over to a nurse, and then Ulrika's friend appeared. Daniel shook her hand. He hadn't caught her name on the phone, and he again failed to hear it as she introduced herself because the nurse was talking and his mind was in a worried fog.

'They've just brought her round,' said Ulrika's friend. 'She looks terrible, but the doctor told me it's all... what do you say? Superficious.'

'Superficial. Thank God for that. Do you know how it happened?'

'A hit and run accident.'

The smiling nurse gestured for him to follow her. He looked at the friend, but she seemed happy to sit outside for a while. The nurse took him into a private room, where he saw Ulrika lying prostrate in bed, without any bandages but with two tubes in her nose. There was, on closer inspection, a heavy pad on the left side of her head. The nurse left him alone. As he sat beside the bed, Ulrika opened her eyes.

'Baby,' he said. 'My baby, I'm here.'

Ulrika smiled weakly and reached for his hand. He could see heavy bruising on her upper chest and wanted to gently kiss it better. She looked ghastly, but at least she was alive and intact. He shushed her when she tried to speak.

'No, darling, don't talk. Just rest. I am here now and I won't leave your side until you are better.'

Jason Ikin's rugby club tour had gone off perfectly, with only one defeat, all-round superb weather, brilliant socialising, top food, and not one arrest, which was a novelty for that particular group of men. The country and the people, in Jason's humble opinion, could not have been more welcoming or friendly. He still held that impression, even though he was battered, bruised and carrying five stitches above his left eye, and missing the final tour match because of it. He had been flattened in the last game and suffered a brief concussion.

He cheered as a penalty try went over for his team, then turned away and burped; too much beer the previous night, and that tripe and garlic soup for breakfast didn't help much. With the match well won already, he wandered off back to the coach. They would be leaving Romania that evening. Perhaps he should rest before they raucously drank their way to the airport. He passed a few pretty Romanian blondes, who had come across from the nearby, grim housing estate to watch the rugby. As he found a seat on the coach, he saw another passing beauty, which made him think of his girlfriend, back home. Then his mind drifted through all the previous women in his life. There had been Elizabeth Johnson, who had died in that car accident. Joanne Haslem, who he still missed, even though she now had triplets and lived with a total moron. And Nancy Niven, of course.

Leo Rooney found a spot to park his vehicle. It was as near to Nancy Niven's building as he could get. He stepped out to the kerb and watched the world go by for a moment. Soon, his date for the day came skipping towards him. She was smiling, dressed in a similar, utilitarian way. It was Gabby, Nancy's friend from the apartment above.

'Hi,' called Gabby, coming to a nervous stop in front of him.

They kissed awkwardly.

'What do you think of the outfit?' Gabby asked, half turning.

'It's just right. Are you excited?'

To be going on a date with you? she thought, starting to grin uncontrollably.

'Come see,' said Leo, taking her back to the trunk. He opened it. His black holdall sat there. From inside, he brought out two automatic paintball guns; top of the range, works of art, which he was clearly proud off. 'There, hold yours.'

Gabby handled the weapon. 'Wow. We're going to have so much fun. Thank you for asking me.' She hugged him and he hugged her back.

30

Every time Kelly spoke to Nancy, whether to simply offer a cup of tea or to discuss something that might be of interest, Nancy had to resist the urge to lunge at the woman's face, to force her to the ground and pummel her with her fists, while screaming that she knew about the two guns. *I know.*

Actually, Nancy amazed herself with how well she managed to keep the secret, and remain composed, even though she was churning inside.

Kelly made a suggestion, although she didn't want to, that she and Nancy should do a big clothes wash; otherwise, the men were in danger of turning into smelly Robinson Crusoe types. It crossed Nancy's mind that if they were to soon starve, then what did it matter about cleanliness? But she agreed, and they spent a morning doing that chore together, chatting quite normally, and then Francesco and Eddi helped them set up makeshift clotheslines between huts on the beach and all the laundry was hung out to dry.

Nancy took a moment to look at the two men. Both were now heavily bearded, and each leaner than when she first saw them on the island. Then, Michael and Ryan, neither wearing a shirt, came down to the beach, on their way to do some fishing. Tommy followed along too, as he never liked to be left alone in the villa. Also, in the last forty-eight hours or so, he had started displaying signs of cabin fever – he was the first male to show that the situation was getting to him.

So, everyone was there, and Nancy felt an almost overwhelming urge to denounce Kelly. To scream at her and point a finger. But, for some reason, she held her tongue. Nancy felt frightened and alone. She looked at Eddi, but he was so sweet, she didn't want to burden him again. Francesco? He was giddily attempting handstands in the sand. No, not Francesco. She wouldn't rely on Tommy to walk a pet dog. So that left the two Americans. Shallow Ryan, or intense Michael. Or maybe both? They could relieve Kelly of the weapons. But what, then?

Francesco had stopped laughing at his acrobatic antics, and stood shading his eyes. 'What is that?' he asked. 'There, near to where the chopper lands?'

Everyone stopped and looked to where he was indicating, seeing square shapes of some sort. They all began to walk over in that direction. They walked in a line, with Nancy going on the furthest right, and holding Eddi's hand. As they got nearer, the forms on the side of the helipad became crates.

'What the fuck?' asked two of the men, simultaneously.

Michael and Ryan got there first. Everyone else stood back, as if near to an explosive device. The two Americans managed to lever one of the crates open, then Michael picked out something and held it aloft.

'Tin of tuna fish,' called Michael. 'Looks like the food supplies we need.'

Ryan kicked another lid off a crate, and brought out a tin of fruit. They all ran to the crates, now highly excited, like kids on Christmas morning. Even Nancy, delighted to know they had food, forgot her worries for a moment and joined in the frenzy.

Eddi imagined his boss, Aldi, back at the restaurant in London, verbally abusing his name to anyone who would listen, for failing to return after taking time off. And then, as far as him being incommunicado, that would be that. He had not been in touch very frequently with his family in Indonesia. Plus, his friends in England were fairly loose, so, basically, he was not being missed by anyone. He had to laugh at the situation, which caused Nancy beside him to glance quizzically at him. They were both eating slices of the apple pie she had baked that afternoon.

'Enak,' he said, through another mouthful. Good.

Everyone was lounging on the sofas, with it raining outside.

'Weather's a bit up and down,' said Nancy.

'Yes, it's the only negative on this once in a lifetime vacation we're having.'

They both laughed.

Tommy was highly agitated, walking about. He dropped his plate in the sink and wandered back amongst everyone, his fists inside his vest sleeves, in that stance that policemen sometimes take. 'Can't we do something?'

'What do you suggest?' asked Francesco, who was lounging on Kelly's chest.

'We could trash the place. Have a massive barney.'

'Oh, a fight?' asked Francesco, sitting up. 'Two teams, perhaps? I bagsy Michael and Ryan. Let's go, you English fucker!' He laughed hysterically, flopping back onto Kelly.

'What about baseball, in the rain?' asked Tommy. A haughty look from Michael killed that idea. 'The go-carts, in the rain? A bigger challenge. Come on, you Italian shit, you crashed off in the dry, have you any balls for the wet?'

Francesco started to rise. 'Fuck you. I've got bigger balls than you.' Kelly pulled him back to her chest.

Tommy persisted. 'Michael? Ryan? The track in the wet? What do you say?'

'Sounds like fun,' said Ryan.

Michael was considering. 'Through the trees it will be pitch black almost. But, fuck, let's do it.'

So, that was agreed upon. Kelly sighed loudly at Francesco breaking free from her embrace. 'Don't expect me to go out in the rain,' she said.

Eddi was keen, too. As Nancy had no desire to remain indoors alone with Kelly, she started to get dressed for the weather.

'What can I say?' asked Nancy, hugging Eddi. 'I'm a motor racing fan.'

Once everyone was dressed properly, they set off through the trees. Nancy felt the rain hitting the hood of her coat. She let Eddi pull her along through the dripping trees, and was glad to get into the go-cart shack, even if she then had to watch the men fuelling and preparing their favourite carts. Suddenly, she was thinking about her daddy, getting very melancholic, before realising that he had once told her about a childhood holiday of his, which involved go-carts and dodgems, at Butlin's holiday camp in Bognor Regis, West Sussex.

The air got heavy with petrol fumes, as the men started to set off down the track. Eddi went off last. Nancy leant over him, shouted for him to be careful, then gave him a push off. The loud noise never left her ears as the men went around the circuit, but Nancy felt alone and cold. She huddled against a wall, bit her nails, pushed her hair back into her hood. Michael came back around first, in the same Number Seven he always drove, giving her a look, before dropping away again, and then it was Ryan rushing through.

Francesco passed through a minute later, calling to her, 'Slippy! Crazy track!'

Eddi chugged through, his bright white smile standing out in the gloom. Nancy waved.

Alone again, Nancy became aware of the wet trees moving all around her in the wind. She started to let her imagination get the better of her, and became more than a little scared. She watched Michael drive round again, then Ryan, then a bigger gap to Francesco and Eddi. The petrol engines drifted off into the rain, but then there came a huge squealing noise and a bang, making Nancy stand up straight in surprise. Then there was almost total quiet, apart from the rain beating on the roof of the hut. She hopped over the barrier and hurried down the slippery track in the direction of the men.

Nancy found it eerie, and quite bizarre to follow the thin strip of tarmac through the bad weather and the ghostly trees. She looked back several times. She thought she sensed things to the left. She was quickly sweating and frightened. Then she heard voices ahead, and saw figures slightly off to the right. Still nearer, there was smoke drifting up into the rain, and she could see three of the men. Finally, she made out Eddi, who turned to let her run into his arms.

'It's all right,' he said to her ear. 'Michael came off.'

'Thank God it wasn't you.'

Eddi giggled. 'I'm fine. Nowhere near.'

Nancy surveyed the scene. Michael was inspecting his favourite cart, now mangled around a tree. She saw that he was covered in mud, with some blood around his hairline.

'Left wheel just sheered off,' Michael said to Ryan.

'Looked nasty from my view. Damn, I was just about to catch you, as well.'

'The fuck you were. Anyway, I've had worse.'

Nancy saw Michael notice that she was there. If he expected her to run to him like a good little nurse, then he had another think coming. Instead, she snuggled into Eddi, and they walked away.

31

As each resident's departure date came and went, the mood slowly started to change in the villa. They had ample supplies once more; they had all the amenities; they had the beach – Kelly and Francesco still had each other, even though they were arguing a lot, but the fun had stopped, conversation died out, people looked at Nancy again, in the way they had done on her arrival.

Out of the blue, one morning at breakfast, Tommy shouted at her: 'What the fuck have you done to make this happen!? What... the... actual... fuck?

Nancy stared at him, before running out to the beach. As Eddi was still sleeping, it was Michael who came out after her, catching her up at the huts. She was trying to avoid crying. She tried to squirm free and walk on, as he pulled her back and embraced her. She wept onto his shoulder.

'They all just want to go home,' he said. 'It's understandable.'

'Michael, I didn't ask for this,' she whimpered, before trying to gather herself. She knew she was a strong woman, and was determined to gain control of her emotions.

He let go of her. He was such an imposing figure standing in front of her, all tanned muscle and tattoos. She was a jumble of emotions. The thought to tell him about Kelly and the guns came to her, but that was all too crazy to put into words. She was suddenly safe with Michael, even though he was one of her least-favourite exes.

'I'm okay now,' she said. 'This will all stop soon. We'll be missed. Someone will come.'

'I'm sure they will. Come on, let's walk in the surf.'

As they walked across the wet sand, her left hip rubbed against his right thigh – oddly comforting. He talked of a few silly things, then reminded her of fun times together in New York.

'Oh, yes,' she remembered, 'the 10k run, where you sooooo wanted to leave me behind.'

He laughed. 'Never. You're cute when all red in the face, with a running nose, and cramp.'

'Oh, sure.'

They reached the far right of the beach, the opposite end to the helipad. Sitting down was as good an option as any. The villa was invisible from that angle, as if they really were the only two humans left on the planet.

She touched the plaster on his forehead, the result of his go-cart losing a wheel. 'Does it still hurt?'

'No, it's fine now.'

'Michael, I thought *you* would have shouted at me first. Not Tommy.'

'That English guy's a bit weak in the head, with no self control. I know you're not to blame. That you don't understand this, any more

191

than any of us do. Keep hanging in there. Something will happen soon, I don't doubt it.'

He was a dark shape next to her, the sun just about blocked by his bronzed shoulder.

'Well, at least it's improved your tan,' she commented.

'Yours, too.'

'Has it? I've not looked at myself recently.'

'I've been looking for you, don't worry.'

She giggled. 'I must look a sight.'

He ran a finger slowly down under the right strap to her top. It caused her to close her eyes at the pleasant sensation. Moments later, he did the same to the other one it seemed like an hour to her between touches, with everything on the island appearing to happen slowly, by then. She wanted him to push the straps aside, but then remembered it was Michael. She sat up, but realised he'd moved on to inspecting her bare waist. If he kissed her there, she would melt into him, but instead she sat with the sun and breeze flowing over her, and he kept looking.

'Strange place,' he said, as if reading her mind. 'I was all busy and rushed in Miami before getting this trip, and now the world has stopped spinning.'

'I suppose we acclimatise to what's around us.'

'I'm acclimatising to the smoothness of your skin. Can I touch it?'

Again, a long, leisurely pause. No rush to go anywhere.

'If you like.'

She had to wait even more as he carried on his visual inspection, and then he even lifted the flimsy material a little bit so he could run a little finger underneath her rib cage. It was the most erotic thing she had felt in ages... well, since Ryan used her in the Love Nest. But the soft touching was so nice, and so unusual from Michael – she always thought of him as... uncouth... no, that was the wrong word. Animalistic, taking and giving furiously. In business and life in general he was calculated and determined, but in his love life he was passionate. But maybe it was the calming influence of the island working on him.

He was running his tongue along the left side of her ribs. A hand was on her lower back, making her arch up to his mouth. He was being patient and gentle, but she did feel like she was back in his New York bed, tied to the headboard, arching her slender waist in ecstasy. Her nipples were aroused, even before her top was slipped above them and his head came up, hovering, then deciding on the left one, to first flick with his tongue several times, and then devour with his mouth, sucking all the perfect, little breast away from her body into a cone shape. Nancy moaned. She was so aroused. So excited. Part of her mind was trying to spoil it; it was arrogant Michael, but she just knew he was going to take her, out there on the beach.

Like a magic trick, her top went over her head, discarded into the wind, followed by his vest, and then her denim shorts were removed by one of his hands, without even being unbuttoned, which made her laugh. There were no panties, which prompted his primal urge and he rushed onto her pussy with his wide open mouth. But he had let himself down a fraction, still wearing his shorts, while she had been fully prepared for a sixty-nine.

Nancy's mouth made a massive O shape at what Michael was doing with his tongue. Then she settled for nuzzling his hairy abdomen, feeling all his stomach muscles straining to get his tongue deeper. Oh, shit, she came simultaneously as some sand was blown across her face, and then Michael was moving into position, her legs were positioned on his shoulders. She had never wanted it with such wild abandon before. She was so ready. She felt his cock slap onto her pussy.

Nancy stumbled back towards the villa. Michael had been gentle, as gentle as he could be with that massive tool, but had just gone on for absolutely ages. The celibate vacation had really built up within him. Her legs were made of jelly, just like her head. She could still see him above her, still smell him, feel what they did, how he had folded her legs back; she was surely bruised by his fingers on the back of her thighs.

She stopped in the foyer, ridding herself of some sand in her hair, and to check she had actually put her shorts back on, so bubbalicious was her brain. She would get a drink, she decided, and head straight to the shower. Noise outside welcomed her return. Kelly was apparently oblivious to it, baking at the stove. Nancy stepped out onto the patio. Ryan was in the shade, playing pool, also ignoring the fact that Francesco, Tommy and Eddi were fighting on the lawn. Nancy ran down there, diving on them, scratching and hitting and screaming for them to stop. 'Stop it! Stop it! You're all fucking animals!'

The melee collapsed outwards, all the combatants just sitting there, panting. Eddi walked off first, a little embarrassed. Francesco took a moment to arrange his hair, while Tommy was checking his teeth, then they got up and departed the scene. Nancy was left there on her knees, emotional anyway, emotional because of making love to Michael, and she cried, out there in the sun. Cried her eyes out.

Eventually, she headed in to go for her shower. She paused near the kitchen, to look at Kelly with disgust. 'You do know your boyfriend was fighting out there?'

'And hello to you,' replied Kelly. 'Me and Francesco broke up this morning. I'm thinking of going for the Indonesian fella next.'

'Fuck offfffffff!'

Nancy went to her room, locked the door and cried throughout her post-Michael shower.

32

Nancy re-emerged into the living area.

Francesco and Tommy had discovered a chess set and were trying to outfox each other across the coffee table – she thought they might as well just play *Snap*. Michael and Ryan were there, but they paid her no heed. Nancy stopped looking around, instead made some tea and toast. She sat with her feet tucked underneath her. Thoughts of betraying Leo came rushing to her; feelings which had been there throughout all the naughty things she had been getting up to, despite her best intentions, and now she felt extremely melancholic. But it was so tough to resist, with all that testosterone flying around, all the history and memories like the way ex married couples can easily fall into bed together, for old times sake.

Eddi wandered in from the garden and sat beside her. She managed to lose her pout, smiled at him, and then put her legs across his thighs.

'How are you?' she asked.

'It's difficult to say. This thing is playing with my head. I still feel like me, but I'm forgetting what it is to be me, if you know what I mean.'

'I think so. I feel... like I'm always being like a bad version of myself. Like the times when I was a difficult teenager to my family. Being made to stay here with everyone is harming the grown-up I became. I hope you understood some of that, because I didn't. It's just stress, isn't it, really? It's a mild torture, wondering if we are going to be taken to our limits.'

'Check!' shouted Tommy, disturbing everyone.

'Really?' asked Nancy, virtually tutting at him.

'What's rattled your cage?' Tommy asked.

'Why don't you do something more productive? Like build a boat.'

'You think I'm sailing away from here with you?'

'No, you stupid man, you go alone. Either find help or die trying.'

Francesco laughed, shaking his head. 'Find help or die trying. Oh, Nancy, I'll come on the boat. We can have fun while Tommy man here rows with the oars.'

Nancy simply looked away.

After lunch, Eddi, Michael and Ryan went to the go-carts. Apparently, with the fuel running out, it was their last playtime. Kelly tagged along to watch from the beach.

'Nancy, come in the pool with us,' suggested Francesco.

Nancy glanced up from her nails. 'No, thank you.'

'Nancy, it is a beautiful day, is it not. Forget all your troubles, forget all the past, we're here, it's still a life. Come and enjoy the pool.'

Nancy looked at him.

'Please, Bella,' he continued, 'I get silly, sometimes. And Tommy man is an asshole. Don't let it upset you. We have to fill the hours while here, so come outside.'

Nancy sighed, got up, and walked away towards the stairs, leaving Francesco hanging. But she went to her room and got into her white bikini.

Tommy and Francesco were already in the pool, attempting a form of water polo, without a net, by the time she emerged into the sunshine. Her pure sexiness stopped them dead, the ball floating away, forgotten. Both men watched her approach, and then admired her sleek entry, head-first, into the water.

She came up between them, so they could both steady her with hands to her hips and elbows until she had wiped her eyes clear of water and got her balance. The water was so warm, and the breeze was a delicious, neutral temperature. Tommy's tattooed left bicep was to one side, and Francesco's beautiful, bright smile to the other. She decided to sit on the middle step, halfway down into the pool, and watch them paddling about. Wiping her hair back over her head allowed Tommy to ogle her arm pits.

'You are so beautiful,' Francesco told her. 'Isn't she, Tommy?'

'Absofuckinglutely.'

Nancy looked down at Tommy. 'Oh, you're liking me now?'

'Celibacy does that to a man,' Tommy replied.

Despite herself, Nancy had to check out the muscles on both men. She wasn't a nun, after all; she was a healthy young woman, surrounded by hunky young men. Guilt over Leo did make her a little unhappy, added to which was the general insanity of the situation, plus Kelly with the guns. But, as Francesco grinned even more, and ran fingers through his wet hair, and Tommy reached for the floating ball, stretching his frame, Nancy felt arousal gathering within her, within her womb. She said to Tommy, 'So, if I do a simple thing like adjusting my bikini top, that would get you hard straight away? Because of the celibacy thing?'

'Nancy, girl, I'm already massive.'

'Oh, but with the... what's it called? Refraction, through the water, it's hardly noticeable.'

'Believe me, it's there. It's so big it hurts.'

Tommy moved closer to Nancy. She imagined him picking her up and easing her down onto his erection. Francesco said something in Italian, which was probably rude. The sun beat down. There was only the sound of the birds in the trees. Nancy, briefly, considered pulling both men up against her, feeling their strength, their muscles, but then slipped between them and started swimming slow breaststroke. Francesco laughed. Tommy went after the ball again.

'Tommy,' called Nancy, 'best to let the blood drain away.'

'It takes a long time to get back down,' he replied.

'Sounds like a problem to me.'

'I assure you, it's not. I'm in full working order.'

'Full working order, yes. But, what are you now, Tommy, late twenties? And no children? Modern men have terrible sperm, I read recently. Perhaps you should get tested.'

'We're never getting off this island, so you'll just have to take your chances, babe.'

Swimming back, Nancy pretended to be shocked. 'You assume a great deal.'

'I remember you used to love my sperm. Couldn't get enough of it. All over your belly or back, on your face, down your throat. Perhaps you've gone off to America and become all posh, forgotten you are just a typical English slag.'

Francesco didn't like that. 'Hey, Tommy man.'

'No, Francesco,' said Nancy, 'it's all right.' She returned to her position between the two men, thinking she had been just that with Michael earlier on the beach. 'Maybe I have become posh. Or just developed a better taste in men. I like to be romanced.'

'Oh, right,' said Tommy, 'so how do you explain getting fingered by Ryan in the tree house?'

For a fraction of a second Nancy was disappointed that her time with Ryan had not remained private, but then the very thought of it turned her on, and her lovemaking with Michael filled her being. She looked at Francesco; she could go with him immediately, just to annoy Tommy. But Tommy was looking so manly, himself, his six-pack bobbing on the water line, his right hand adjusting himself down there amongst the blue trunks. Before she knew it, she was snogging Tommy, hands to his face, feeling herself lifted like a doll, her wet body against his. Nancy came off Tommy's lips and tongue for some air, sensing Francesco still closely there. The man was not embarrassed in any way, just grinning. She felt the urge to touch his face, so she did. 'Oh, Francesco, I can't leave you out.'

So Nancy and Francesco kissed. His left hand slipped inside her right bikini cup, fondling her. She switched to Tommy's mouth. Tommy was fiddling with his side of the bikini top, revealing soft flesh which he took his mouth to, allowing Francesco back to tongue Nancy deeply. Nancy was completely gone, lost in pleasure, forgetting everything. She felt magnificent Tommy through his shorts, and he had been telling the truth. Francesco moved to suck Nancy's right nipple, pausing only briefly to laugh and say, 'Threesome!'

'Not here!' said Nancy, trying to cover herself.

'What does it matter?' asked Tommy, sounding frantic.

'My room,' she gasped.

Tommy came up a step and she was suddenly faced with his cock to work with her hand, and Francesco followed suit, offering his long manhood to her other hand. She played for a while. Nancy went down on Tommy first, giving as much attention as she could muster, still manipulating Francesco. Then she swapped over. One of the men removed her bikini top and she then felt the enormous excitement of having them both fondle her breasts. Tommy removed her bikini bottoms while she was kissing Francesco. Francesco was on her, his solid chest dominating her, while she cupped his tightly contained balls. Francesco got out of the pool to kneel beside her; she watched his amazing nudity, noticing particularly his slightly hairy chest and his muscled abdomen. Of course, he was cradling his manhood, and Nancy had to prepare to receive his cock into her mouth again, which distracted her from Tommy rubbing his tip up and down her slit, before he buried himself balls deep up her. Nancy's eyes went wide at the amazing violation but she was unable to speak. It all quickly became intense, both men giving it to her; Nancy's ankles were put on Tommy's shoulders, Francesco was groping her breasts as he worked himself in and out of her mouth. Nancy turned her eyes to see Tommy sweating and concentrating on his task. She was experiencing something so amazing as to block out any rational thoughts over it.

And it was going on forever.

The forever suddenly stopped as her holes were withdrawn from. Dizzy with ecstasy, lost in pleasure, Nancy felt Francesco turning her onto her hands and knees beside the pool, its aqua beauty reflecting on her face, the sun briefly burning her bare bottom until Francesco was in position, finding her from behind simultaneously she was gagging on Tommy's sticky member, and it started all over again. She could imagine Francesco with his hands on his hips as he fucked her, occasionally sweeping back his hair, grinning widely. Tommy had hold of her hair at the back of her head as he fucked her mouth. She knew it was crude, but loved every second of it. She was just that typical English slag. She had a terrible thought of the two men high-fiving, but then Francesco pushed so deep that she lost her mind again.

'Spit-roasted,' said Tommy.

33

Nancy came down the stairs after a very long shower. A very long shower, indeed. She hated herself, at least a little bit; just a little bit, mitigated by the odd circumstances in which she found herself. She felt battered and weak-kneed, but also exhilarated. Naughtily pleased with herself, in fact.

She looked nervously into the lounge area before entering. Only Eddi was present, sitting with a mug of tea while reading one of Kelly's novels. He looked at her with a perfectly normal expression, but she imagined his great disapproval; in fact, his face briefly morphed into her distraught, disappointed father.

'I'm not happy,' Eddi said.

Nancy flip-flopped over to make a cup of much-needed tea. 'Are you not?'

'No, we've run out of petrol and the go-carts are finished with.'

'Oh, well, never mind. I bet we'll be out of here in a week.'

'How do you figure that?'

'We're all so far beyond our vacation dates that someone, somewhere, must have raised the alarm. That will go through the various levels until some policeman starts checking up.'

'Will you come to see me in London, after all this?'

'Of course, Eddi. God, I'm running to my family after this shambles.'

'Home to England?'

She joined him on the couch. 'Yes, home to England.'

Francesco passed through the lounge, freshly showered and dressed in black. He and Nancy ignored each other. Nancy snuggled over into Eddi.

'I bet you miss your restaurant kitchen in London,' she said. 'Isn't all that pressure addictive?'

'True, it is, I can't wait to get back to it. Perhaps I should have cooked here more.'

'No, you were letting everyone else have free reign in the kitchen. It was very nice of you. You're so sweet.'

'You're the sweet one, Nancy.'

'If only that were true. Hey, I'm sorry if I've neglected you these last few days. Let's hang out together now until the end.'

Eddi smiled happily at her.

Kelly came sprinting in from the garden, 'Helicopter!' She headed out the front door. 'Helicopter!' Then they could hear it passing over the villa. Ryan and Michael came jogging after Kelly.

'What now?' Eddi asked Nancy, hauling her to her feet.

'Shall we go and see?'

'Well, we're not too busy, are we?'

They giggled, held hands, and followed the others.

'Where's Tommy?' he asked.

'You know vain Tommy, when he goes for a shower he stays in for hours.'

Nancy and Eddi wandered down to the beach huts and palm trees. The two Americans stood there watching the helicopter lifting off and heading out to sea. Kelly was kicking sand in her frustration at missing it. Then everyone realised that there was a figure kneeling near the helipad: a man, messing with his holdall, before standing, looking around, shouldering the bag, and heading in their direction.

Kelly threw up her hands, 'Now who the fuck is this!?' She walked back to the others, looking specifically at Nancy. 'Nancy, obviously something to do with you, do you recognise him?'

'I'm sorry, I seem to have forgotten my binoculars.'

The new man slowly plodded across the sand. He was clearly young. Nancy, her mind still a bit frazzled from the day's erotic events, tried to wrack her brains; there weren't that many men left in her past. *Were there!?*

The man was wearing a black vest and jeans. He was well-built and tanned. He began to walk backwards so that he could savour the sea breeze coming in clearly he was there for a holiday, not to do anything in an official capacity. Finally, he turned back to them.

'Jason!' cried out Nancy, running to him.

A stunned Jason Ikin dropped his bag to accept Nancy into his arms. Everybody looked at each other.

'Any idea who he is?' asked Ryan.

'Nope,' answered Kelly, 'but it's nice to have a hunk here, at last.'

Michael smirked at her before heading back in. Ryan went, too. Eddi watched as Nancy, minutes after swearing to be with him for the rest of their time there, stood in front of the newcomer, gently touching his face.

'Let's go back, as well.' said Kelly. 'Come on, Mr Indonesia 2016, let them get reacquainted.'

Kelly and Eddi turned their backs and headed up to the villa, Eddi looking back once.

'I've been waiting for youuuuu. Oh, thank God, you're here at last!'

Nancy and Jason were sitting on the beach, where they'd met. He kept gesticulating with his fingers, trying to decide what to say, but his mind struggled to comprehend the situation that she had just explained to him.

'Let me get this right, Nancy. All those people are your exes? Wow, I mean, you know me, I won't turn my nose up at a free holiday. I'm only late because of my rugby club tour. But... whoah.'

'There's Tommy, as well.'

'Another one? Christ. Why? What's it all about?'

She shrugged.

Nancy had already checked his bruised face from his rugby injuries. Then she just stared at him, so relieved to have genuine, amazing Jason there – the regular guy, the salt of the earth, builder Ex from back home.

'Are you going to introduce me, then?' he asked.

'No.'

'No?'

'It's all a bit weird here now.'

'Bloody hell. What have I got myself into this time? So, I've got an awkward fortnight before the helicopter comes back for me?'

'Helicopters don't tend to come back, Jason. That's the weirdest thing. That's how messed up it all is.'

Jason put his hands to his head. 'I'm lying to my girlfriend for this, you know.'

'Jason, I'm sorry.'

'Wait a minute, there was a girl in that group.'

'Mmmm.'

'A girl? Was that before me? Yes? Why did you never tell me?' That fun fact was relaxing him a little, and he grinned. 'You could have told me that.'

'Just a silly college thing.'

Jason's face dropped. 'Which one did you dump me for?'

'Non of them, Jason. It was never like that.'

'Anyway, what a fabulous place. Leaving aside the insanity of it all, absolutely beautiful. I'm knackered after that flight.'

'Well, let's go in. I'll feed you and find you a room.'

'I'll have to say hello to those guys.'

They got to their feet and headed in.

'If you must,' she answered.

Jason Ikin woke up and thought he was still in Romania. Slowly, as he yawned and stretched, it all came back to him: Nancy Niven, with all her exes, in the Caribbean, stranded like Robinson Crusoe. Well, sort of Robinson Crusoe. Shiiiit!

He sat up, remembering the lukewarm welcome from the other people, as if he were a spare cock at a wedding. His fault, he supposed, for coming in late. The big English guy, Tommy, asking if he intended drinking any tea, like it were oxygen itself, answering that he drank coffee, and then the handshake was forthcoming. All the men with beards, like it were some charity fundraiser *Didn't they pack razors?* The spare woman looking like a prostitute. At least she asked if he had a nice trip.

He swung his legs out and sat up further, in the room next to Nancy. Bloody Nancy Niven, unbelievable. He thought he was over her. With a groan, due to his injuries, he got up and headed to the bathroom. Under the shower, he concluded, now that the shock had passed, that he was still happy to be there. He was young and always ready to enjoy himself. Perhaps Nancy had been melodramatic about the lack of return helicopters. He would have to see.

The sun was high in the sky, so he decided that he had slept all the way through to the afternoon. Walking into the living area, wearing his three-quarter length shorts and a white Firetrap vest, with black mules, he moved amongst all of Nancy's exes, and they were a bit more civil to him. He made conversation, while trying to place them in a time frame of Nancy's love life. Eddi took him on a tour of the kitchen.

Kelly called from a sofa, 'You'll be on the cooking rota soon.'

Jason smiled and nodded. He was more interested in Eddi.

'You're Indonesian, Eddi?'

'Yes, I am.'

'So, you know Nancy from..?'

Nancy wandered in from the garden, joining them in the kitchen. She watched Jason making coffee. 'My two men,' she said.

Eddi smiled wanly, then moved off.

'Come outside,' Nancy said to Jason.

They stepped into the sun and Jason assessed the vacation

playground. He would be in the pool soon, no doubt about that. He looked Nancy up and down, in a sarong and tight black top, showing some amazing cleavage, with her hair in pigtails.

'You look lovely,' he told her.

'Thank you. You look as handsome as ever, even all beaten up.'

'What a place? I could never afford to stay here, even with a big gang of mates. You must have enjoyed it?'

'Somewhat, I suppose. After the realisation of being here with those people and then up to a certain point. Now I'm desperate to go.'

He pointed to the love nest. 'What's that? A tree house? Let's go in there.'

Nancy was reluctant, but followed him up the ladder. Jason thought it the coolest place ever, settling down, looking out to sea. Nancy joined him, looking at the vacant space that had been filled with Ryan touching her intimately.

'Right, Nancy. You must have some idea what's going on. There must be a logical reason behind it all.'

'I honestly don't know. I don't know how or why my exes were gathered together.'

Jason finished his coffee, put the cup down. He deliberately took Nancy's hand, as if to say "well, Jason's here now to look after you" and they both watched the empty sea spread before them.

34

Nancy insisted that Jason should experience something of what the villa had to offer, so she sat watching him swim. Then he had a game of tennis with Francesco, where he heard about the ski town of Madesimo for the first time.

'A chalet maid?' Jason asked of Nancy, letting a ball hit him. 'Really?'

'Yes, really.'

'Did you have to wear a uniform?'

'Of course not. Play on.'

Francesco enquired about Jason's time with Nancy in England but Nancy interjected with a warning for him to behave. Francesco came up the court to volley a winner, paused as the shot bounced off the side fence, then asked, 'Jason, man, did you do a threesome with her?'

'Francesco!' shouted Nancy.

'I'm sorry!' laughed the Italian. 'I'm sorry. Deuce.'

Later, there was a little session of baseball catch with Michael but Michael was clearly not the type of man to reminisce about his time with Nancy. Then Kelly had prepared cocktails on the terrace. For Jason, the happy-go-lucky builder from Luton, it was easy to forget the strange circumstances surrounding him. He drank whatever was offered to him and sat in the shade. Soon, it was tea time, with more alcohol consumed. Then he found himself lounged out with Nancy's feet over him, talking to Ryan about rugby and their mutual liking for crime drama box sets.

As the evening went on, Jason told Nancy about his girlfriend, Annie. Nancy expressed happiness for him. She told him about Leo Rooney, to which he nodded warmly. Nancy remembered how her sister had recalled the time that she bumped into Jason on a job.

'Oh, yeah,' he recalled. 'It was lovely to see Lucy again. I would so date her, if she wasn't your sister.'

Nancy giggled. 'I'll be sure to tell her.'

'So, are you going to remain in New York, with this Leo?'

'Well, I will stay in New York because that's my life. Leo is amazing, but, well... he's not exactly rushing to save me, is he?'

'You don't know that. He could be very worried. He could be on the job right now.'

'We'll see.'

'Well, my Annie is great. But she's so busy it will take another month before she realises I'm not back. I assume you've explored the island?'

Nancy gave a deep nod, sleepy from the wine. 'All alone. Yep. There are other villas, though. One we think is for honeymooners.' That made her remember what she had discovered of Kelly's behaviour, with regard to the guns. Perhaps Kelly had just found them in the other villa, and it was all innocent. But still Nancy knew she was in denial about the subject. Perhaps, after a good night's sleep, she would mention it to Eddi and Jason. Men would know better what to do about a situation involving guns.

The morning came, and she was frolicking in the surf with Jason, all thought of the guns out of her mind again. She hadn't noticed at the time, but Eddi had watched them go, disappointment etched on his face.

Everyone was down on the beach: Kelly sunbathing, Michael and Ryan exercising, Francesco and Tommy making a sandcastle, shouting when the Americans' feet came too near to their six-turret masterpiece. Eddi was wandering about on his own, kicking driftwood.

Nancy came out of the water, attracting all eyes. She squeezed her hair out over her left shoulder, wiped her body a bit, then lay down near Kelly, only because there was a towel there.

Kelly glanced over at her. 'You're having a nice time.'

'That's one way of putting it.'

'He's very cute. A builder, is he? He can put an extension in for me any time.'

'You do know he doesn't like you?'

'Yes, I got that impression.'

They watched Jason hop out of the surf. He was pulling his shorts up. He was alive and refreshed, most surely not giving a moment's thought to the situation.

'Hi, Jason!' called Kelly, waving.

Nancy turned away. 'Stop it.' She found Francesco and Tommy

watching her. Knew that they were thinking about the threesome. She turned back, ready to smile at Jason, but he was talking to Ryan and Michael.

'Hey, Nancy!' called Tommy, standing up next to his sand art creation. 'What do you think of my castle?'

'It's fabulous,' she called, over her shoulder.

'It's got six turrets.'

'One for each year of your mental age.'

'What are you being like that for?' He turned to a standing Francesco, appealing to him, 'Fucking women, eh, Frankie?'

Francesco shrugged in agreement.

Both men approached Nancy. Tommy said, 'You weren't so up yourself during our threesome.'

Kelly took notice of that. Nancy ignored him.

'Hey, Nancy,' said Francesco. 'Be nice. We'll do it again, yeah?'

Nancy hissed, 'Go away.'

Tommy visibly reddened around his neck. 'If the opportunity presents itself I bet you won't be able to resist.'

'Well, we'll see, won't we.'

'You're only good to be spit-roasted.'

Jason was there, enraged. 'What did you fucking say!?'

Nancy jumped up, surprised by Jason's approach. 'It's all right, Jason. He's full of crap.'

Jason was livid. Tommy was not exactly happy, either. During a stare-fest between the two men, with Nancy trying to intervene, they closed the gap between each other.

'What did you say?' repeated Jason.

Fuck you, man! I was talking to the—

Jason's fist came over the top of Nancy's right shoulder, catching Tommy on his left eyebrow, sending him backwards with a spurt of blood. Jason ducked from a screaming Nancy's grasp to get back in front of Tommy, landing three more punches before Tommy could get one off. Another left cross put Tommy spark out on the sand. Francesco had been about to get involved but thought better of it.

Ryan ran over to intervene. Instead, he turned Tommy over into the recovery position. Michael stayed watching from a distance. Eddi started to walk back, aware that something had happened. Nancy pulled Jason away, and they went up to the villa.

'Wow,' said Kelly to Francesco, 'That was like being at home in England on a Friday night.'

In the evening, nothing was mentioned of the fight. Tommy had been patched up, and didn't seem to hold a grudge against Jason. He just wanted his beer and another game of chess with Francesco. Nevertheless, it was clear that Jason was going to protect Nancy's honour from then on, much to Eddi's chagrin. The Indonesian wandered about most of the night before retiring early. Nancy did stand to hug him, watched him mount the stairs, then she returned to Jason's side.

Nancy didn't need any man standing up for her. But she did appreciate Jason's actions. His heart was in the right place.

Michael sat down nearby in his dressing gown after a bath. Nancy watched him drinking tea. After a moment she noticed that the MG initials on his dressing gown were different from the MK on his mules. 'Hey, Mr MG,' she said, causing Michael to face her. 'What's the MK?'

'Oh, not mine. They're a pal of mine's at the tennis club. Must have swapped them by mistake.'

'Ah.'

Jason wanted her attention, so she leant in to him and giggled at what he said. 'You naughty man.'

35

On his first day in Stockholm, Daniel had gone to a café near the hospital with Ulrika's friend. Having overheard a nurse call the woman Alice, he was pleased not to have to ask her name again. Alice knew nothing about the hit and run accident but, seeing as Ulrika was likely to make a full recovery, it wasn't that important, she thought. Daniel agreed, although he just had to get over his impotent fury against the person responsible. It turned out that Alice was an old school friend of Ulrika's, a resident of the city and, although very pretty, not in the modelling industry. She thought it was wonderful that he had dropped everything and rushed to be at Ulrika's bedside. She also told him which of Ulrika's relatives were on their way – some he knew, some he didn't. He supposed it was a silver lining on a terrible event, getting more involved with his lady's family.

Afterwards, Alice had left for home, promising to return when she could, and Daniel wandered around the shops by himself, picking up toiletries and snacks. Despite the circumstances, he was happy to be back in Stockholm, taking a great interest in all the people going about their daily business. He planned to go to Ulrika's apartment later to shower and have a rest, but for then, he headed back to the hospital.

He had to wait for Ulrika's doctors to finish a visit, then he joined her, kissed her forehead, and settled in for the night, holding her hand and talking whenever she was awake.

The following few days took on a pattern for Daniel, staying in Ulrika's flat, then being at the hospital while she was treated, and undergoing minor surgery on a knee. Ulrika's mother and two female cousins had arrived, and had been very friendly towards him. Ulrika was recovering well, even telling him to return to New York, worried about business. But he would not leave her. He kept in touch with the office. Everything was fine.

One foggy morning, he took a break from the hospital, walking to a nearby coffee shop. Again, he watched the locals, wondering if he would be spending more time there in the future. He glanced through a copy of a local newspaper while sipping his coffee. The Nancy Niven situation was in the back of his mind, but he kept forcing it down. Zach, in the office, had enquired of her whereabouts through his secretary, apparently. When he got back to New York he would look into it. No doubt Nancy would be back at work before he was.

He left the coffee shop, skirted around a woman with two dogs, and headed back in the direction of the hospital. It was quite chilly in the fog, people rushing about in the gloom. He crossed the road, thinking about Ulrika and her long-term recovery, looking forward to caring for her in their New York apartment, and he didn't even hear the car gun its engine and deliberately drive into him with such force that he was dead before his body landed on the tarmac.

Nancy woke up in contact with his manly back. Sleepily, she turned her lower body into his rock hard naked buttocks and sighed contentedly. Her thoughts were a mixture of the previous night's lovemaking and the wild dream she had just emerged from.

Her eyes opened. She could smell the unmistakably beautiful scent of Jason Ikin. She raised up a fraction. Then she remembered their seemingly natural and inevitable coming together. *Wow.* Maybe it had been the second chance between the two of them, the finding each other again, but it had been absolutely amazing.

Jason stirred, turned. She let him turn over onto his back, pleased to see his morning wood, its tip sitting half in his belly button. Her hand moved to his balls, warm and tight, lifting, eliciting a groan. Her other hand lifted the heavy shaft, and her mouth slipped over the end.

Coming downstairs, Nancy was faced with the obvious development that Kelly was now with Michael, as her old friend's hands were all over Michael's ass and they were trying to get their tongues down each other's throats. The fact that it was being done with Francesco watching nearby seemed inappropriate to Nancy, but she tried to ignore one more absurdity of her vacation, and moved towards the kettle.

Nancy felt a poke in the back, swivelled to find Eddi beside her. She touched his arm, seeing if he was all right. He nodded, though he was clearly a little down, and Nancy was not so stupid as to fail to connect it with Jason taking over her affections.

Eddi indicated the new, odd couple. Nancy made a disappointed mmm noise.

'To the garden?' he asked.

'Uh-huh. Right there.'

She made her tea and followed him out. They sat on loungers in the shade. Eddi started to speak, but raised voices from inside the villa stopped him. Instead, he said, 'Looks like Francesco was waiting for privacy before he kicked off.'

'What is Kelly doing? Why complicate it even more?'

Eddi grinned. 'You can talk.'

Nancy had to smile at him. *It was what it was, but no one got hurt. Kelly obviously doesn't give a damn about anyone's feelings. She just wants to be Alpha female.* She sighed. 'It is so beautiful here.'

'You're so beautiful.'

'Just on the outside, maybe.'

He tutted. 'Nonsense. Hey, Nancy, why don't you, me, and Jason, take supplies and move to the Honeymoon villa?'

'The Honeymoon villa? We'd have to change its name. Wow, what an idea. Getting away from here. But I'm not sure, Eddi. When the authorities come, we should all be together. Don't you think?'

'I think I've given up on that, to be honest.'

Nancy moved over to embrace him. 'Oh my, Eddi. Don't despair.'

Jason appeared, yawned, and was not the least disturbed to find Nancy and Eddi embracing.

'So?' asked Jason. 'What's on the itinerary today? A tour of the local monastery? Para-gliding?'

Eddi released Nancy. 'I think you and I should play tennis.'

'Eddi, you're on. Just let my breakfast digest.'

So, a little later, the two men played a few games of tennis. Nancy declined to watch, and instead she wandered off, ending up in the Love Nest to look at the sea. She settled down, but quickly realised that it wasn't going to be the tranquil, relaxing experience she expected, because, if she craned forward a little bit, she could see Michael and Kelly going at it like wild animals on the sand. *God, was that what I looked like with him?* Kelly's feet were flailing around in the air, her breasts moving up and down, Michael's buttocks thrusting, with his shorts down to his thighs, which suggested it had been a spur of the moment thing.

Nancy found it hard to tear her eyes away from the show. She felt something akin to jealousy, watching Michael turn Kelly, find her from behind and pound into her, causing Kelly to toss her hair and drag her fingers through the sand.

Nancy heard a giggle from below the hut. She looked down through the hatch where she saw a smirking Tommy, jostling scowling Francesco with his elbow. Tommy looked up at her and grinned.

'Hey, Nancy,' said Tommy. 'Are you being a naughty girl watching too?'

Tommy climbed up, followed by Francesco.

'Do you mind?' complained Nancy.

'Frankie, better view up here.'

Nancy wanted to leave but there was too much muscle now blocking the way.

'Oh, look at the boy go,' continued Tommy. 'Really giving it to her. Is it getting you horny, Nancy?'

'Move.'

Francesco was in a sulk. 'His technique is crap.'

Tommy slapped him on the back. 'Yes, she's an idiot, Frankie.' He turned to Nancy. 'Oh, look, Nancy, totally balls deep now. That must be getting you wet. Mind if I check?'

'Fuck off.'

'Don't be like that, babe.'

Tommy was up against Nancy.

'You're about to lose your sight,' she warned him, raising her talons.

Tommy clamped her against him, with his hands on her bottom.

'Get the fuck off me.'

'Oh, come on, Nancy, feel how much I want you. Frankie here wants another threesome.'

'Fuck offff!'

'Hey, guys!' It was Michael calling up to them. 'Helicopter about to land!'

They all strained to see the helipad. Tommy still had hold of Nancy's buttocks and his erection was against her side.

'Get your fucking hands off me, Tommy.'

Tommy let go. 'Sorry, babe. Only playing. Come on, this could be the end game.'

They all descended from the Love Nest and walked after Michael, with Tommy trying to make his cock comfortable. Kelly was off running towards the helicopter again. On this occasion she got as far as having to spin away from the whirling sand as it lifted and departed. She was livid, kicking out at imaginary things.

Nancy shaded her eyes and looked across the beach, seeing Kelly's obvious distress, and then watched as she pulled herself together and greeted yet another arrival. Nancy's stomach fell, not sure that she could take another Ex showing up. Surely they were down to platonic school boyfriends, by then.

Nancy sat down right where she was, resigned to her fate. She let the sun sit on her closed eyes, sensing quiet as the men went out to meet the newbie, and then gradual noise of conversation as they brought him in.

'Hello, Nancy,' said a familiar voice.

She opened her eyes, but it was hard to see, apart from the shapes of everyone around her. She shaded her eyes, leant away from the sun, trying to make out who it was. She got to her feet. Slowly, under a corona of sunlight, she realised that, *obviously now*, she was face to face with Gus Kaitiff. Nancy found the grit to step up to him and slap his face hard; then she turned and ran.

36

Nancy fled towards the villa. *Stupid! Stupid! Stupid!* Where had her head been? *Stupid, stupid bimbo! Of course it was him.*

Having Gus there; the nausea rose inside her, both because of his arrival and for her subconscious decision to take the easy way while on the island and not remember him. Because she had been happy that he wasn't there, she had closed her mind to the man. She slowed her run and took deep breaths. Was she being hard on herself for not seeing what was right there in front of her face?

Into the lounge, seeing Jason and Eddi relaxing after their tennis match caused tears to gush from her eyes. Both guys jumped up and received her torrent of panicked words. 'My rich ex, called Gus, New York, I should have known he was behind it all – oh God, we have to go. Yes, we'll go to the Honeymoon—'

Jason took her by the upper arms. 'Nancy, calm down, girl.'

'Jason, Eddi, please, I can't be here any more.'

'Someone else is here?' asked Eddi.

'Please, Eddi, we'll go to the other villa. Now.'

Jason and Eddi conferred with their eyes.

'We leave now?' Jason asked Eddi.

'Take supplies from in front of everyone?' replied Eddi. 'Are we asking for major trouble? They outnumber us, two to one.'

Nancy was crying. 'Oh, please.'

Jason held her tight. 'Nancy, we'll go tonight. In the early hours. Take supplies and sneak away. Between now and then we'll keep you upstairs.'

'But, Jason..?'

'We'll stay with you. We won't let anything happen to you.'

'Yes,' put in Eddi, 'Let them think you're just shocked. It's the right idea.'

Nancy allowed them to rush her up to her bedroom before the others returned.

Ryan had been swimming in the sea, and arrived back at the villa after the new arrival had been quizzed by the others, brought up to speed, and had a cup of coffee made for him. At first, Ryan gave the impression of being excited, to see a really old guy standing there must surely mean an official had arrived on the island to organise their repatriation to the States.

'*What?*' he asked, when told by Tommy who the man was. 'Another one? That fucking ho.' Nevertheless, he took Gus's strong handshake when it was forthcoming. Then stood back to observe the scene alongside Tommy. They saw the man was in a white shirt and khaki shorts, with sandals. There was an expensive, heavy gold watch. His hair was slicked back in that Rich Man way, like the actor, Michael Douglas. And he was already tanned.

Ryan went for a glass of water, finding himself near to Michael. 'So, another face.'

'Yeah, man,' answered Michael. 'Well, when we move into the cannibalism stage, we'll eat the new fucker first.'

'That's a deal for sure.'

Gus took a stroll about the living area, looking out at the view. He was being friendly and gregarious, complimenting Kelly on her appearance, discussing "soccer" with Tommy, and recounting a trip to Rome to Francesco. It was all: "well, well, well, I have a little fling with some younger woman in New York, and end up getting invited to a most unusual set-up. Extraordinary".

Tommy decided to bring up the obvious, that Nancy and her splinter group were excluding themselves. 'Nancy's less than happy to see you, Gus.'

'True. That's very true, Tommy. I admit it was sometimes a difficult relationship with Nancy. Perhaps it was the age gap. Was she pleased to see each one of you fellas?'

Tommy laughed. 'Definitely not.'

'Then we are in the same boat, my friend.' Gus turned to Kelly. 'Kelly, would you be so kind as to show me the grounds?'

Kelly was happy to do that.

Tommy watched them stroll out, chatting. 'Well, enough of that, I'm starving.'

'Me, too,' said Francesco, going to the kitchen with him.

Michael and Ryan shrugged, then moved away.

Jason and Eddi were doing their best to keep Nancy calm, but she was like a caged lion, thinking everything round and round in her head, pulling her hair and breaking cups and shampoo bottles, etc, until she was exhausted and collapsed on her bed. While Eddi stayed upstairs, Jason went down to collect some food and drink to get them through the evening. He only bumped into Tommy, telling him there was no problem, just that the arrival of Gus had been the final straw, that Nancy was emotionally shattered. That she would be all right in the morning. While Tommy wasn't looking, Jason took the torch that was under the sink and put it in his pocket, thinking it would be needed for their departure. Also, he saw the spear gun, which Ryan had used a couple of times, standing in the corner, and kept that in mind. Satisfied that Tommy would express all of what he had told him to the others, Jason took sandwiches and coffee upstairs and the three of them settled in to await everyone else going to sleep.

The evening turned quite cool. They chatted about many things, some of no importance, but also of how things would be at the Honeymoon villa. They could hear the others downstairs, getting a little boisterous. Nobody came up to mediate, not that anybody was expected to.

'Guns,' Nancy suddenly said.

Jason stirred from his position on the floor. 'What?'

'Guns. Two handguns. Kelly brought them back from the other villa.'

Eddi sat up in his chair. 'Nancy, what do you mean?'

'Me and her walked to the other villa that time. I had cause to look in her bag for something. Saw that she had found or collected two guns. I never challenged her over it. But now I think she's working with Gus.'

'What exactly is your relationship with this Gus?' asked Jason, standing. 'I could see that you didn't like him. That he freaked you out. Who is he? A fucking gangster, or something?'

'He's a rich guy. He's mad. He was a mistake. Oh, God.'

Eddi was still puzzling over the guns. 'Why have Kelly bring them in?'

'Well...' thought Jason aloud, 'He had them brought to the island, but he's not going to bring a weapon through Customs himself.'

'So, he'll be armed by now,' pointed out Eddi.

Jason looked at him. A bizarre vacation was one thing, but this was heavy shit. 'Eddi, now, as far as they're concerned, we'll be down in the morning. Maybe he won't be doing anything crazy just yet. Anyway, we're out of here by 2am. Sounds like everyone's drinking down there. Eddi, here's the plan. I'll go down at 2am, get as much food as I can. You stay with Nancy until I come and get you, and then we head out.'

Eddi nodded his agreement. Nancy rolled over on her bed and hugged her pillow, watching her two best men.

Nancy fell asleep. It was a relief to Jason and Eddi. She actually slept through quite a raucous evening downstairs, all no doubt fuelled by alcohol. Finally it went quiet about 1am.

Nancy sat bolt upright, checking they were still there. Jason moved over to hold her. 'Not long now,' he whispered.

They gave it another forty-five minutes, to be sure; then Jason slipped out of the bedroom and crept downstairs. There was moonlight, so he held off using the torch. He found the mess of a wild party, glasses and bottles strewn about, chairs overturned. He moved as silently as possible, only pausing when he felt stickiness underfoot. Here he used the torch, finding what he thought to be blood stains. Then he heard snoring, and clicked off the light source. It was Tommy, asleep on one of the sofas. His face was buried in the cushions. Jason stepped into the kitchen area, found an old potato sack and quietly filled it with as much foodstuff as he could. Finally, he took a large knife from the block, put it through his belt at the back, and picked up the spear gun as he left.

Back upstairs, they were fully dressed and waiting for him. Eddi was wearing Nancy's rucksack. Jason handed him the spear gun. Then Jason touched Nancy's cheek before leading them out.

They went out the front way, moved around the side, intending to pass the Love Nest and head away past the race track, and then up into the jungle. Jason had the torch ready to use once they were clear of the villa. Suddenly Eddi was on the floor with a big expulsion of air. Jason and Eddi steadied him back to his feet. They looked to see what he had fallen over. Nancy gasped and grabbed for Jason. It was a man's body. Jason aimed the torch and switched on. Francesco lay there, dead as a doornail, his lower face covered in blood. Jason did check for vital signs, finding none. On closer inspection, he could make out a terrible gash from ear to ear. He briefly moved the light away, fearful for Nancy, but she was already burying her face in Eddi's shoulder.

'Was he killed with a knife?' asked Eddi.

'Yes,' answered Jason.

'What's wrong with his face? A broken nose? Maybe it was just a fight.'

'More than a fight.' Jason illuminated Francesco's face again.

There seemed to be no nose. Realising that Nancy was looking, he plunged them into near darkness again and moved them on towards the trees.

37

Jason, Eddi and Nancy stumbled through the jungle all night, with just the torch to show them the way. Nancy thought about poor Francesco the entire way, and hoped the money he'd been paid would find its way to his family in Italy. Finally, they reached the Honeymoon villa as the dawn was just showing in the sky. Nancy was physically and emotionally exhausted, so she crashed out on a sofa, hiding her tear-stained face in a pillow. The two men immediately set about barricading the front door with furniture. Then they made sure the water and power was supplied, and made coffee.

Jason made Nancy take a cup of coffee, then he and Eddi stepped out onto the pool decking area, which was smaller than the villa they had just left. The pool was oval, with an infinity design overlooking the sea view. There were bushes on two sides forming part of a property boundary. A pool house stood to the left of the pool.

'You're bleeding,' pointed out Jason, indicating Eddi's face.

Eddi touched a cut which must have happened as they trekked through the jungle. With his long hair, scruffy beard, and spear gun at his side, he imagined he looked like one of his Indonesian ancestors.

'So, we're here,' said Eddi. 'To what end? Just sit here and wait for them to come for us? You think they'll come?'

'I think so. That's what it's all about, after all. Would you prefer to stay out in the jungle?'

'No, but what can we do to protect ourselves?'

'I'm thinking about that one. Give me a minute.'

Eddi spent a minute looking at the sea, sipping his coffee. 'Well?'

Jason grinned, and slapped Eddi on the shoulder. 'Let's look upstairs. See what the field of sight is, if we keep watch in shifts. Maybe we can barricade ourselves upstairs.'

'This is fucked up, man!'

Tommy was in a highly distressed state, storming from Michael to Ryan to Gus, and back again, with Kelly sitting on a sofa with her head in her hands. Tommy stopped at Gus and pointed at him. 'You arrive, and the same day, the *very* same day, Francesco gets his fucking throat cut. Come on!? For fuck's sake!'

Gus remained impassive and offered up his hands. 'Not a mark on me. You were arguing with him last, as I remember.'

'Everyone was arguing with everybody else last night!' Tommy put his hands on his head in desperation and turned away. 'Oh, Christ. This is so bad.'

'Tommy! Shut up,' pleaded Kelly. 'I can't think straight.'

'What's to think about, you stupid whore?'

Kelly sprang at Tommy with her nails out, screaming abuse, but Michael caught her and spun her around.

Ryan was rubbing his face with both hands. 'Look. Who's not here? There's a murder and then people go missing. That's more obvious than it being Gus.'

'Whatever!' shouted Tommy. 'It doesn't matter, anyway. We're totally fucked, man! Nobody is coming for us and now we—'

Gus had pulled a gun and shot Tommy dead through the forehead, coldly and calmly.

'Enough,' was all he said.

It silenced Kelly, stilled her to the core. Now, for the first time, she really knew what she had got herself involved with. She had collected the guns. She was complicit with a man's murder.

Gus turned his gun towards Ryan, but Ryan had already bolted for the door, his fleeing form blocked by Michael and Kelly. Gus looked at Michael. Michael looked at Gus.

'Michael,' said Gus. 'He's all yours, son.'

Michael let go of Kelly. 'Yes, father.' He drew his own gun and ran in pursuit of Ryan.

It was just a quivering, shocked Kelly and a cold-blooded Gus left in the villa. He was fondling the gun. Then his eyes lifted to her.

'So, Kelly. You've met the boss now. Me.'

'What are you going to do to me?'

'Well, little lady, I'm considering a bonus for you. Or maybe an extension to your contract. What would you like, Kelly?'

'I don't want anything, thank you. I didn't sign up for this.'

'You don't want anything?'

'No, sir.'

'I'm afraid I *do* want something.'

'Oh, what?'

Gus looked her up and down. 'Bedroom. Now!'

Ryan had tried to be clever, even through the adrenalin rush in his panicked mind. He had not fled straight into the jungle, but instead had grabbed the baseball bat and waited just around the corner of the villa. As soon as he heard someone running after him, he pounced out and swung the bat. Michael raised his arms on instinct, taking the blow mainly on his left shoulder. His gun flew across the lawn. Then they were grappling for dear life. It was wild, base, like cage fighting without the cage punches and gouges and knees going in – a raging, sweating maul of a fight. Michael got on top and immediately went for a nose bite, causing Ryan to scream out. From somewhere deep inside, Ryan managed to roll Michael, and was kneeing his side, causing great expulsions of air. Then more fists were exchanged before Ryan was flung off. He had remembered the direction in which the gun had gone and scrambled for it. Michael tripped him at the ankles. Ryan kicked backwards, cutting Michael's face.

Ryan stood with the gun in his right hand. He was exhausted, terrified, unused to holding a gun. Michael knew he was beaten, standing there panting, waiting for Ryan to find the nerve to shoot.

A gunshot rang out, startling the wildlife nearby. Ryan fell to the left, shot dead through the right side of his neck. Michael spun around. There was nobody else there. But then he saw his father upstairs on a bedroom balcony, gun in hand.

Michael cleaned himself up and put a Band Aid on the cut from Ryan's boot. He leant over the sink in the kitchen, drinking water. He felt no pain from the fight yet, but was fuelled up and ready to carry on with the plan.

Gus came downstairs, his gun in his waistband, his shirt open down the front, revealing white chest hair. He ran a hand over his head, his expression showing the intensity of the morning's work. He looked at his son as if noticing him for the first time.

'Kelly?' asked Michael.

'She no longer works for me.'

'Are we going now?'

'No rush, son. No rush. I think we should eat first. I've bought all this food, after all.'

38

It was dusk when Gus and Michael approached the Honeymoon villa in a wide arc, coming from inland. They slipped into the compound through a gap beside the pool house and the hedge. There was nobody outside. They crept over to the open doors of the living area.

They could see it was gloomy inside. They stood still and waited, and listened, let their eyes adjust. Gus indicated things out to Michael with the point of his hand gun. Michael made out shapes on the sofas. He had been expecting a violent scene to match the one with Ryan, had built himself up for it, but maybe they could finish it while everyone was sleeping.

They made the advance slowly inside. In a flash, Jason slashed at Gus's gun hand with his knife and got it up to the man's throat and, from the other side, Eddi rose to his feet and had the spear gun pressed to Michael's shocked face.

Nancy rushed forward and almost sank to her knees with her desperate, wailing question, 'Whyyyyyyyyy!? Why do this!?'

Nancy recovered her posture. She was crying, but furious. She wanted her two men to follow through with their weapons. She hated the two Americans so, so much.

'Why?' she asked again. 'Why?'

Gus was the one to answer. 'It's simple, my dear Nancy. A woman can leave a Kaitiff man. Such is life. But the same woman cannot leave two Kaitiff men. It simply cannot happen.'

'Oh...my...God.'

While the insanity of the whole thing sank in, Michael had gradually moved his gun hand until he was sure he would hit Eddi's leg if he pulled the trigger. He imagined that spear pinning him to the wall as a result, but he had to do something. He fired, filling the room with a white flash and a bang, before Eddi fell away in agony, the spear gun dropping to the ground. Gus reacted and began wrestling with Jason. Nancy screamed with rage and threw herself at Michael, scratching his face. Eddi had hold of Michael's left leg, which allowed Nancy to avoid being easily pushed off.

It was a shambolic scramble of bodies and fists and curtains coming down. And Eddi gushing blood over the floor which had Michael slipping. Nancy was like a limpet on Michael's face, gouging his flesh. Gus was down on the kitchen floor, his gun loose. Jason was punching the older man, with his knife hand held off. Jason used all his muscles from rugby and punched through the strong defences of big man Gus. Finally, he felt the man sag down to the floor.

Nancy was batted away onto her backside by Michael. 'No!' she screamed, as Michael aimed his gun at Eddi's face and pulled the trigger. No white flash that time, it jammed instead. Eddi pulled

Michael down on top of him. Michael began to pummel Eddi's face with the butt of the gun. Blood spurted. Bone cracked. Nancy screamed.

Then Nancy stumbled across the floor and her hand alighted on the spear gun. She brought it up, aimed at Michael and fired. Everything went suddenly quiet, as Michael reached up to the spear which was fully through his throat, and then he fell away.

Jason, gasping and bleeding, was at Nancy, pushing the spear gun out of her hand and getting her up. He just wanted out of there, which was understandable. They went to Eddi. Eddi's wound was in his right lower leg. Quickly, Jason made a tourniquet out of a towel to try to stem the bleeding.

'Get Nancy out,' gasped Eddi.

'We're all going, pal. Nancy, help me get him up.'

They lifted Eddi, and Jason put the smaller man over his shoulder in a fireman's lift. They went out into the night. There was no logical thought taking place. No reason apart from leaving that scene of violence. They moved down towards the beach, seeking a place to put Eddi down. It was rocky down there. They found a secluded stretch of virgin sand and lay Eddi on the ground.

Now they were able to regroup, deal with all the extreme emotion of what had just taken place. Nancy sank to her knees, horrified at killing someone, yet proud of her decisive action in saving Eddi. Jason checked on Eddi, who seemed bright, despite his multiple wounds. Then Jason inspected his own bloody fists. Adrenalin was seeping away and he felt shattered.

'Jason,' said Nancy. 'Thank you. I'll always love you.'

Jason's hand was to his mouth, but he nodded at her.

'Will you always love me, too, Jason? Tell me.'

'Of course, babe. I was just counting my teeth.'

Nancy managed a giggle. Then she sank back into melancholy, watching the lovely Eddi. All of that violence and insanity because she rejected Gus and his son, Michael. Without ever knowing they were even related. How bizarre and sick.

Eddi grimaced with pain, bringing Nancy back to the present, and she got up to go to him. It was then that she saw Gus stepping towards them, gun advanced ahead of him, and she gasped with terrified despair. Jason jumped to his feet.

Gus, battered, his chest and shirt blood-soaked, his face a mask of pain and hatred, stumbled towards them. His final act would be to finish the whole damn thing. He aimed the gun at Nancy. His finger began to squeeze the trigger.

From nowhere, Gus was floored, easily disarmed, screaming with pain, with Big Ronnie, the Tae Kwan-do Black Belt from New York, kneeling on his back. Nancy felt like she was in a dream. *Big Ronnie there!* Then she laughed with sheer, unadulterated relief. She turned around, looking for Daniel Bridgford. Daniel had surely come for her. But, instead, she saw her little Zachy, her friend and PA from the office, stumbling towards her over rocks, wearing a bright orange life preserver. He looked so out of place. Behind him were men in black military uniforms. There was the sea, with a small military craft beached.

Big Ronnie smiled at Nancy, as if he did that kind of thing every day. 'Hello, Miss Nancy.'

'Ronnie, darling.'

Then Zach reached her and she hugged him with all her

remaining strength.

'Are you all right, Nancy?' Zach asked. 'Please tell me you are all right.'

'Zach, darling, I'm all right.' She kissed him. 'You came for me.'

'I did, didn't I? I'm quite the hero.'

Nancy watched as the Navy men began to tend to Eddi. She smiled at Jason. And then she hugged and hugged Zach again, who was crying his eyes out with relief.

39

New York City, 18 months later

Nancy's hard hat was grey and without a peak, which made her feel a little bit like a German paratrooper in World War Two, except that it also had her name emblazoned on the front.

It was a Monday morning, and she was at a warehouse conversion in Tribeca, showing around a young, rich couple from Hong Kong, who were trying to find a base in New York. The apartment they were looking at was currently a shell, but the space was very generous, and the pair had the chance to have things laid out to their exact taste while the work was going on.

Nancy took a moment, letting Mr and Mrs Cho move aside to confer. She appraised the woman, seeing a pleasant, if rather plain face, but also fabulous long legs which Nancy envied. Oh, the couple had a little kiss, having to hold their own hard hats in place while they did so, which made Nancy smile.

Resuming her career in New York had been a tough decision for Nancy to make. Her family, after the trauma of getting her back safe to England, wanted her to stay home in London. Following her attendance at Daniel's funeral, then the intensive police investigation and subsequent trial, with media frenzy, it would have been easy to rebuild her life in London. But, anyway, there she was, working for a new firm, loving what she was doing once more, with her hero, Zack, moving with her as her PA.

Gus Kaitiff was convicted and locked away. Eddi had recovered well from his wounds, and was back home in Indonesia. The nightmare was slowly being put behind Nancy. She still got flashbacks, but was standing very strong through it.

'Can we see the penthouse now, please?' asked Mr Cho, disturbing Nancy's reverie.

'Of course. Of course. There are builders at work, but we can venture up there. This way, please.'

They walked up the stairs, making small talk. The noise of building work greeted them, then there was more light and Mr and Mrs Cho were even more taken with the layout. Mrs Cho, who so far had been quite shy, turned to Nancy and smiled broadly.

'Nancy,' said Mrs Cho, 'can we have this floor and the floor below? But we would want them to blend together more, and we have a lot of little requirements?' She looked at the paperwork she carried. 'Could we say twelve million dollars for both, done to our specifications?'

Nancy smiled back at Mr and Mrs Cho. They all giggled. Then a builder stumbled through the scene, in a hard hat, dirty white vest, denim jeans and a utility belt hanging like a Western gun belt.

'Oh, excuse me,' said the builder, in a British accent.

Nancy looked at her boyfriend, Jason Ikin, but didn't speak to him. They exchanged the slightest of amused looks.

'Mr and Mrs Cho, you keep looking around, carefully, while I make a phone call. Okay?'

Nancy moved around a concrete pillar, her cell phone in hand. Jason came from the other way, and they took the opportunity to hug and kiss.

'Jason, I'm working here,' she giggled.

'So am I. Kiss me. Babe, I love you.'

'I know. I love you, too.' They kissed deeply. 'Right, get off me. Shoo. Get back to work.' Jason moved away, grinning. 'Cheeky man.'

Nancy watched him go, then dialled a number.

Nancy and Jason shared an apartment in The Bronx. Since leaving the island, they had become inseparable, and she had helped him secure a job in the construction industry. His current contract happened to involve property that she was handling. Jason had taken easily to the American way of life; New York excited him, he liked the people, the food was amazing, and he had become a basketball fan, following the Knicks.

Nancy came back to collect him from the Tribeca development later that day. She picked him up in her white Porsche Panamera. That make and model of vehicle did, at first, keep taking her mind back to Gus Kaitiff, but she had decided not to let that man take away her love for a Porsche, after all.

It was a warm and sticky New York day, and with Jason being all dusty, they showered together. They laughed as they washed each other's bodies. Jason was exactly what she needed after the horror of the island. What you saw with Jason, was what you got. A real, down to earth Englishman. Their love had rekindled so easily. Soon, she hoped, they could finally forget the past, and move forward completely, maybe even to starting a family.

Jason's kisses aroused Nancy easily. The water jet was hitting his hard shoulders and sending a warm mist across them. His huge erection stood as a barrier between their bodies. Jason helped her hop into his arms, his big hands holding her by her cute ass, and she slipped down onto him without even a guiding hand. He took her roughly up against the tiled wall, the jet striking down on her gyrating chest. 'You are mine!' he was saying, over and over, and she was answering in the affirmative.

Afterwards, they made dinner and settled down to relax. They chatted about each other's day. He suggested that they go to the English pub on the next block, while she suggested an early night.

While Jason washed the dishes, and then sat down in front of the TV to watch *Major League Soccer*, Nancy got on with some paperwork. She also checked her mail. She was intrigued to see a letter from the law office which had represented her through all the trouble. At first, she was apprehensive, as she ripped it open, then puzzled. She focussed and read it thoroughly.

'Jason,' she said, entering the lounge area. She had to wait while a free-kick was taken and the effort ridiculed by Jason. 'I've had a letter from the lawyer people.'

'And, babe?'

'We've had an offer from a television company to do interviews about what happened.'

Jason turned off the soccer. 'What kind of offer?'

'A two million dollar kind of offer.'

When he worked in England, Jason always did the National Lottery, and imagined not going to work if his numbers came up. Working with his brother did lessen the joy of telling a boss to stuff their poxy job, but nevertheless he did long to be in that position. But, the following morning, feeling exactly that way, he had gone off at the usual time to continue with the Tribeca building.

Nancy kissed him, then leant on the closed door after he had gone. They had talked into the early hours about the offer, until they had both fallen asleep. Of course, he wanted the money. It was only being interviewed, after all. But Nancy wanted nothing to do with it, any more. Yes, the cash would set them up for life, but she was doing so well, already. She just wanted to put it all behind her.

She finished getting ready for her first appointment of the day, and was just about to leave, when she decided to open her laptop and *google* the presenter on the show which wanted them to appear: a lady called Abbi Riverside: a thirty-year-old blonde, originally from Texas, with a background in news reporting, with this show being her breakthrough on a major network. Then Nancy looked up any link between Ms Riverside and the name of Kaitiff. On finding no results, she went to work.

Nancy and Jason were sitting in the office of her lawyers' Entertainment and Media branch, on Manhattan, with a very slight view of Central Park; which Nancy tried to put a value on in her head. Nancy was in a cream business suit, her hair in a high ponytail. Jason looked very uncomfortable in a grey suit - she kept having to make him stop pulling his collar out. Their new lawyer, Helen Harbaugh, came back into the room, smiling.

'Yes,' said Helen, retaking her seat. 'Ms Riverside's representatives are in the building. Let's go through things in more detail, before we sit down with them. So, it will be a series of interviews until they are reasonably happy that the... situation has been covered. They will cover all transport and accommodation costs. The preliminary schedule is three working days, not counting travel time. They want to interview you with the villa in the background, which they have hired, and overnight you will be staying in the villa...'

'Whoah!' said Nancy, raising her hands. 'I understand I have to return to the island, but I'm not sleeping in that villa.'

'Oh..?' said Helen. 'Right. Having looked at the geography, I'm not sure they can shuttle you back and forth. Perhaps they can get what they need in one day? Let me go and say hello to them, and raise that little issue.'

Helen smiled again and left them alone once more. Jason took hold of Nancy's hand.

'Was I wrong to say that?' Nancy asked.

'Of course not. I don't want you there. We'll see what they say.' He smirked a little. 'I just want my million dollars.'

Nancy laughed. 'I know you do, darling.'

'I love you, Nancy.'

'I love you, too.'

'I'll be with you all the way. We'll just answer their questions, let the programme get made, then get the hell out of there.'

Nancy nodded. They kissed.

Helen returned, still smiling, obviously happy in her work. She retook her seat.

'Right, then,' said Helen. 'They'll be brought through soon. They say they can hire a boat, a motorised yacht, which will take yourselves, and Ms Riverside and her assistant, to the island. It will moor offshore, and you can retire to that as the filming goes along.'

Nancy was relieved. 'And Eddi?'

Helen checked her paperwork. 'That gentleman is *en route*, as we speak. And I believe you know that your personal assistant, Zachary, and the martial arts person, Big Ronnie, will be arriving by helicopter, with the crew. So..? Are we good to bring in the other party?'

Nancy sighed deeply, then nodded. 'Yes. Please do.'

40

In the Bahamas, Nancy and Jason stopped dead in their tracks on the dockside, and stared at the massive, white catamaran-style yacht which was to be their transport back to the island.

'Bloody hell,' said Jason, admiring the three-tiered boat, with wide access walkways at both sides of the stern. 'I'm sure I've worked on that, back in Stevenage. The client would drive his Bentley up that side and down the other.'

'Isn't it beautiful, Jason.'

'It's expensive, babe.'

They continued to follow the local man with their luggage. They had been brought straight from the airport. The sun was hot, but the sea breeze was wonderful, giving them a vacation feeling. That sensation was added to with the appearance on deck of a tall, blonde woman, wearing a sarong, sunglasses on her head, with a long drink in one hand and waving with the other.

'There she is,' said Nancy. 'Pretending she owns the thing.'

'Try to be nice, darling. Smile and wave back.'

'Hello,' called Abbi Riverside. 'Come aboard!'

Nancy led the way, and was first to receive the obligatory air kisses.

'Hey, great to meet you two, at last!' said Abbi, in her Texas drawl, which Jason fell in love with instantly. 'I'll make you a drink. We're sailing without much crew, I'm afraid. Had to leave the cocktail waiter back in New York. What would you like? Jason, what do your tastes stretch to?'

Jason wondered if that was a double entendre, then let his mind drift to a pint of *Tetley Bitter*, but replied, 'I'm sure we'd love what you're having.'

Nancy smiled at the save from her man, as Abbi spun away to throw together more drinks at the bar. Nancy had taken in the very straight blonde hair, and the even straighter teeth. Abbi was close to six foot tall, something that always managed to intimidate the petite Nancy. She was, at least, pleased that Jason was looking off across the harbour, and not at the imposing American lady.

'Thank you so much for agreeing to all this,' said Abbi. 'It's not so scary once we start. We'll become friends, and then we chat; you'll forget my people are even filming.' She passed them their cocktails. Jason sniffed his dubiously. 'Nancy, you left originally from here, am I correct?'

'Yes, I did, Abbi.'

'Oh, please, y'all sit with me. I'm not sure these are real leather couches, but I'm happy to be here, I can tell you.' Abbi looked them over, as any journalist would, seeing the real people, not just the names behind a story. 'So, yes, my film crew, and the "lesser" guests, are over at the heliport right now, about to set off.'

They looked over, perhaps half a mile away, to a less salubrious part of the docks, spotting two red helicopters sitting on their pads, with people milling around.

'Amazing boat,' said Jason.

'Isn't it just? I've put you two in the front cabin. You'll find your luggage in there, after we depart. Well, you look very tanned and healthy, Jason. Are you still working with your hands?'

Jason nodded, sipping his drink.

Nancy asked, 'Ms Riverside...'

'Abbi, please.'

'Abbi, do you need to ask me things? I'm ready, you know.'

'Oh, honey, not yet. You just sit back and relax. We shall all become friends. I've told the captain to take a circuitous route, so we won't get there until late tomorrow sometime. I want you both relaxed and at your ease. It will make what I've got to do easier.'

They were joined by a tanned man in a black polo neck sweater and black trousers. He was drinking what looked like mineral water. He smiled, but Nancy failed to feel any genuine warmth from the man.

'This is Malcolm,' introduced Abbi. 'Malcolm is one of my most trusted people.'

Malcolm shook hands with both Nancy and Jason, then took up station on the stern rail.

Then the captain of the yacht clambered barefoot down onto their deck. Abbi introduced him by the name of Phil. He wore a white sailing cap and polo tee shirt and shorts; he was about forty, and reminded Nancy of her father. He welcomed his new passengers warmly, then asked permission to depart. His accent was hard to place.

'By all means, skipper,' answered Abbi.

Phil touched his cap and moved forward along the edge of the boat, gesticulating to crew on the dock.

'The skipper is from New Zealand,' Abbi explained. 'That's a beautiful place.'

'Oh,' said Nancy.

'Wait on,' Malcolm suddenly said. 'What's this coming now?'

They all looked to where he was pointing. A figure was jogging along the shoreline towards them. It was a bulky, unusual looking man, and as he got nearer they could see he was in a baggy red tracksuit and open-toed sandals.

'Big Ronnie!' exclaimed Nancy.

Abbi looked perturbed, clearly not happy to have her arrangements interrupted in such a manner. Nancy stopped her from calling to the man by explaining about his eccentricities. Then she stood to the rail and waved.

'Ronnie!' called Nancy.

Ronnie came to a stop below the boat. He didn't seem to be out of breath at all. 'Miss Nancy! Permission to come aboard.'

While Malcolm clearly tensed, Abbi brought out her most professional smile. The imposing martial arts expert came up on deck, apologising profusely.

'I'm sorry. I'm sorry. Please forgive me, Ms Riverside,' said Big Ronnie. 'But I'm glad I caught you. Lovely to see you, Nancy. Jason, how are you?' Handshakes took place between the two men. Then Big Ronnie passed Nancy a small, leather shoulder bag. 'Your seasickness tablets, Miss Nancy. You know how you get.'

'Oh, thank you, Ronnie, you're a darling.'

'And some of your favourite sweets in there, as well.'

'Thank you.'

They kissed.

'Is Zach with you?' asked Nancy.

'Yes, yes, he's over there, pining for his husband.'

'Is that it?' asked Malcolm. 'Only that the captain was about to... shove off, you know.'

'Yes, yes, I'm sorry,' apologised Big Ronnie again. 'I'll get off. Disembark, so to speak. I'll see you out there, Nancy.'

He and Nancy hugged. Then he jogged down to the dock. Moments later, the yacht moved off. Everyone waved to Big Ronnie. Even Malcolm raised his hand.

The yacht headed slowly out to sea. Nancy sat back down. She looked in the bag and brought out a packet of humbugs, which she offered round. Jason took one, while Abbi and Malcolm politely declined. They moved slowly past the heliport where Nancy could make out the waving figures of Zach and Eddi. She frantically waved back for as long as she could.

'My first time on a boat,' said Jason, excited to feel the boat pick up speed, off the coast.

'Oh, really?' asked Malcolm, without a change in expression.

Jason looked at Nancy, wondering if the man was being funny with him, but Nancy shook her head. She wrapped her man's arms around her and they began to enjoy the open sea.

'I love you,' Jason whispered to her right ear, causing her to giggle.

Nancy sighed back into his chest. 'I wish you weren't here, darling.'

'The money. Remember the money.'

'I know, I know. I just wish you were safe in New York, and not involved with this.'

'Nancy, you're involved, so that means I'm involved.'

Nancy let her mind drift ahead. One way or another there would be closure. There would be... other people were on the boat! The sound of voices below deck. Nancy was at first alarmed, then she heard a woman laugh naughtily. Perhaps it was friends of Abbi. A wooden door opened and, wearing shorts, giggling and trying not to spill his champagne, surprisingly came the heavily tattooed form of Leo Rooney. He was pulling along, in a black bikini and also carrying a champagne flute, a giddy Gabby, the ex-friend of Nancy who had stolen Leo from her when she needed him the absolute most.

Nancy was dumbstruck. Leo and Gabby lost their party mood in an instant. Nancy lunged for Gabby's face, but Jason easily restrained her.

'What the fuck!?' demanded Nancy. Her eyes flared at Abbi Riverside.

Leo appeared quite sheepish, embarrassed to be caught playing with Gabby. 'Hello, Nancy,' he said.

Jason was ready to spring around Nancy and punch the American. 'Don't hello Nancy her!'

Abbi came near, letting the scene unfold as if it were in front of her cameras. She was ready to intervene, but Nancy asked the vital question.

'Why are *you* here?'

Leo put down his glass. 'Nancy, I believe I'm the unreliable boyfriend who failed to come to rescue you. That's what it says in my contract for this show. And Gabby is the reason I failed to do that.'

Nancy stared daggers at her ex-friend, who was deliberately looking out to sea.

Abbi did interject, 'There's only so much room on the helicopters, Nancy.'

Nancy felt panic rising, as if she were back on the island. She tried to stand, but Jason held her back. 'No, no, Jason. I want to go to my cabin.'

So Jason helped her to stand, and they edged past the embarrassed couple of Leo and Gabby, now holding each other. Abbi indicated for Malcolm to guide Nancy and Jason, and the three of them went below decks.

41

Jason cuddled Nancy in their cabin until the shock of seeing Leo had started to leave her body.

'Leo Rooney... with us on the boat,' she said, sitting up, fingers dragged roughly through her hair. 'And her... with him, too.'

'Stop it now, Nancy,' he admonished. 'Listen, I can throw them overboard for you, if you like, or you can be cool about it.'

She giggled. 'I'll be cool. It's just one day, after all.'

'Good. Now, are you ready to go out there and face them up?'

'Face them up? Jason, baby, you want me to intimidate them?'

'Well, not really, I'm just keen to know where the champagne's at.'

They both laughed and fell about the bed. She let him kiss her everywhere.

But they did decide to go back out on deck. He pulled her to her feet. She hitched up the little bag at her hip.

'Do you want to leave that here?' he asked.

'Noooo, it's from Big Ronnie. I want to wear it.'

'Okay.'

There was no land to be seen anywhere around when they went topside, with Nancy's hair flying wildly in the wind. Leo and Gabby were sitting in the stern with just Abbi for company.

'Hey, you two,' welcomed Abbi. 'What, no swimming costumes? I can't wait to see you in trunks, Jason.'

'Any chance of a drink?' asked Jason.

Abbi indicated for him to feel free at the bar. Jason found the champagne and supplied himself and Nancy with a glass each. They sat themselves down. Silence. The journey was clearly going to be very awkward, indeed.

Nancy woke in Jason's arms. She had to think hard to remember where she was, but the rhythmic moving of the bed was quite a good clue. The previous evening came back to her: the seafood meal and the wine, and the nonexistent conversation, although Abbi had not stopped trying to flirt with Jason. They had retired early.

She kicked off the sheet, as it was very warm, and the sun was streaming through the slats covering the porthole. She stood to look out, seeing that the boat was barely making any progress; Captain Phil no doubt obeying instructions to take his time getting them to the island. Bare female legs walked past the window: Gabby's legs. Nancy pulled a face.

'What's happening?' slurred Jason, stirring to shade his eyes.

'Put your shorts on. I think we're sunbathing today.'

Jason used the tiny but luxurious shower, then put on a pair of pale blue *Calvin Klein* swimming trunks. He slathered himself in sun cream, did his hair, found his sunglasses, and then said with a smile, 'Good to go.'

Nancy laughed at him and leant over to peck him on the nose. She was in a maroon bikini, flip-flops, and with the little leather bag across her chest.

Jason grinned. 'That's like one of those microphone packs on *Big Brother*.'

Nancy slapped it to her hip. 'I love it. Makes me feel safe thinking about Big Ronnie. Ready?'

'Yep. Can I get a bit pissed?'

'No, you can't get a bit pissed.'

They went on deck, greeted by the only other crew member, who they had met the previous evening; his name was Aaron, and Nancy thought him to be quite sweet.

Malcolm was sunbathing, his face impassive under his mirror sunglasses, so they moved past him, up onto the forward deck area, watched over by the smiling Captain in the wheelhouse.

'Good morning!' welcomed Abbi, wearing an off-the shoulder beach playsuit, in several pastel colours. Gabby was sitting nearby, in what seemed to be the same outfit.

'Look at us,' continued Abbi. 'Abbi and Gabby, the fashion twins.'

Nancy gave Gabby a cursory glance, before looking at the sky, which currently had one solitary cloud covering the sun, but it would soon be glorious again. She was deliberately ignoring the tattooed form of Leo Rooney, in white shorts, who was doing a Titanic pose on the prow of the yacht.

Jason went for the nearby coffee and croissants, saying a brief hello to Abbi when she reached out to touch his forearm. He sat with Nancy, away from the American – he usually liked older women, but that one unnerved him. He and Nancy cuddled up and enjoyed the sensation of being far out at sea.

'Well, isn't this nice?' said Abbi. 'Such a relief to be out of New York.'

Nobody felt like replying, so she went to help herself to another cup of tea.

Leo joined them. He was very toned. His confidence was back. Nobody gets tattoos to that extent without possessing great inner confidence. Nancy looked up at him, while Jason deliberately did not. There was chemistry in the air that would explode into violence if Jason would just have stood up. Leo moved away and took his seat beside Gabby. Gabby's stern expression, and pout, suggested that she was thinking about her TV fee, wanting the situation to change. The sun came out again.

Nancy remembered having once seen a photo of bikini-clad beauties dancing on the stern of a yacht in Monaco harbour. After an afternoon of sunbathing, drinking champagne and eating canapés, she was done with the playgirl lifestyle. Having to watch the occasional fondle of Leo's bicep by Gabby, or listen to Abbi talk to Jason, her mood had deteriorated.

'I've got a headache,' she said to Jason. 'I'm going down to the cabin for a while.'

'Okay, babe. Do you want me to come, too?'

'In a bit.'

Nancy went by Malcolm, still in the same spot. She wondered if he had quietly died of a heart attack. She entered her cabin, or what she thought was her cabin, but she had gone the wrong way down the corridor and she had walked in on Leo, visible using his shower. Nancy caught her breath. She hadn't noticed him leave the deck. She saw the great body, the ink work, the flaccid yet impressive member with soapy water cascading from it. Leo turned his face to look at her.

'I'm sorry, Nancy,' was all he said.

'So am I.'

Nancy backed out and found her own cabin. She showered, then collapsed in just a towel onto the bed.

Perhaps half an hour later, Jason came in. They kissed and swapped expressions of love.

'Did Abbi molest you when I left?'

'No, surprisingly. She was chatting with the weird Malcolm fella.'

'Let me get dressed,' she said.

'Okay, I shall watch you.'

'I'd be offended if you didn't.'

She put on a tee-shirt and shorts, and then the little bag in place, solely that time to make a big deal of positioning the strap between her breasts, making Jason smirk. Nancy laughed and was about to flop down on him again when there came the sound of two dull bangs, in quick succession.

'Have we hit something?' suggested Jason.

'I don't think so.'

They got up and headed out of the cabin. That's when they heard Gabby scream, and they stopped dead, Jason against Nancy's back. They realised there was nowhere to go but up on deck, to face up to whatever was happening. The yacht had stopped, just wallowing in the swell. The sun beat down. Malcolm was no longer in his place.

Cautiously, they headed forward.

Nancy gasped, seeing young deckhand Aaron lying on his face, his white shirt soaked with his blood. Then she took in the scene before her: Captain Phil lying in a grotesque and bloody position, shot dead. A horrified Leo and Gabby were standing, being covered by the handguns held by both Malcolm and Abbi.

'See, Malcolm,' said Abbi, turning her gun on Nancy and Jason, 'I told you the sound would carry.' She waved them a little nearer.

Leo was protesting in a panic. 'What the hell is this!? What are you doing this for?'

Gabby was a quivering wreck at his side.

Nancy could feel Jason straining to act, to do something, but she held him behind her.

Gabby spoke up, 'Please, what is this all about?'

Abbi looked to Nancy. 'Can you work it out, Nancy?'

'I'm guessing that you're continuing this on for Gus Kaitiff,' said Nancy. 'I looked you up, but there was no link. Who are you, his Goddaughter, or something?'

'No, no, I am his daughter. Only recently found through a DNA test, though. It's a total secret. So...'

'So?'

'So, when you freaked out going back to the island, and massacred everyone but me and Malcolm, before shooting yourself, there will not be any connection to be found.'

Malcolm moved towards Leo, almost in slow-motion, put his gun to the man's tattooed neck, and fired one shot. Leo collapsed sideways over the guard rail and fell into the sea, causing Gabby to scream, and continue screaming until she choked and sank to her knees, gagging.

'Malcolm!' admonished Abbi, looking over the side. 'That was careless to do that.'

Nancy was stunned to see Leo murdered right in front of her eyes. Her heart was going crazy inside her chest. Her ears were so full of frenzy and pumping blood that she couldn't hear Jason's horrified moan of despair beside her.

But she kept her brain functioning. She could see Abbi watching Malcolm move towards the helpless Gabby; she would not be falling overboard when shot in the head, she would remain as evidence. The man raised his gun up slowly. From inside Big Ronnie's bag, Nancy brought out her own gun, and fired four or five shots wildly towards the wide target which was Abbi and Malcolm. One bullet luckily struck Malcolm in the head, sending up a fine mist of brain matter, before he collapsed onto the again screaming Gabby.

Abbi, shock now etched on her face, fired her gun twice, in a reflex action, before she realised that she had been shot in the abdomen, and she sat down on the deck, the gun falling aside.

Nancy checked Jason over in a panic, but he was unscathed. He was just totally stunned.

'Oh, thank God,' she said. 'Thank God you're okay.'

Jason stared at the gun in Nancy's hand, but he made no move for it. They both approached Abbi, who was drenched in her own blood. They made no attempt to offer her any kind of First Aid.

'Babe,' said Jason, 'You got Big Ronnie to bring you a gun. I can't believe you did that. You expected this?'

Nancy nodded, and allowed her man to embrace her. 'The money is safe, darling. I made sure of that. We have Kaitiff's money, at least. I just knew something was wrong with all this.'

'You amazing girl. My crazy, brave girl.'

Nancy kissed Jason. Then she moved across towards old friend Gabby. She picked the girl up off the deck and they held each other very close.

After a minute, Nancy returned to her man Jason, and they hugged and hugged on the rolling deck.

Hope Izzati